finding perfect

finding

PERFECT

ELLY SWARTZ

FARRAR STRAUS GIROUX

New York

Farrar Straus Giroux Books for Young Readers
175 Fifth Avenue, New York 10010

Copyright © 2016 by Elly Swartz
All rights reserved
Printed in the United States of America by R.R. Donnelley & Sons Company,
Harrisonburg, Virginia
Designed by Kristie Radwilowicz
First edition, 2016
1 3 5 7 9 10 8 6 4 2

mackids.com

Library of Congress Cataloging-in-Publication Data

Names: Swartz, Elly D., author.

Title: Finding perfect / Elly Swartz.

Description: First edition. | New York : Farrar, Straus Giroux, 2016. | Summary: "With some
help from her siblings and friends, Molly is able to face her OCD and be strong enough to
get help for it"—Provided by publisher.

Identifiers: LCCN 2015036347 | ISBN 9780374303129 (hardback) |
ISBN 9780374303136 (e-book)

Subjects: | CYAC: Obsessive-compulsive disorder—Fiction. | Emotional problems—Fiction. |
BISAC: JUVENILE FICTION / Social Issues / Depression & Mental Illness. | JUVENILE
FICTION / Family / General (see also headings under Social Issues). | JUVENILE
FICTION / Social Issues / Friendship.

Classification: LCC PZ7.1.S926 Fi 2016 | DDC [Fic]—dc23

LC record available at http://lccn.loc.gov/2015036347

Our books may be purchased in bulk for promotional, educational, or business use. Please
contact your local bookseller or the Macmillan Corporate and Premium Sales Department at
(800) 221-7945 ext. 5442 or by e-mail at MacmillanSpecialMarkets@macmillan.com.

For James, Joshua, and Gregory—
You make my heart smile every day. I love you.

finding perfect

1

blue pixie and the
siamese fighting fish

MY COWBOY BOOTS SCUFF the wooden floor as I walk onto the stage, and for the next ninety seconds I won't think of anything but the rhythm and sound of each syllable in my poem. Today is Round One of Lakeville Middle School's Poetry Slam Contest.

The applause comes to a slow stop. I spin my lucky sea glass in my pocket one last time as I tap the microphone. My best friend Hannah gives me a thumbs-up from the fourth row. Still not used to her new hair. I actually like the black-as-night-tipped-in-blue pixie cut, but the uneven bang fringe isn't really working for me. She said she's paying tribute to Fred, her blue-flecked Siamese fighting fish that died two weeks ago, so I told her I loved it.

The crowd stares at me. Waiting. My mind quiets. I love this moment. The Before. When everything is still and anything is possible. I take a beat to look out at the faces, and then the words flow as I march across the stage.

Sorry
Bad timing
like a broken clock,
a flat tire,
the blare of a police siren when you're trying to sleep.
I say okay
just bad luck
like a black cat,
Friday the 13th,
an open umbrella on the kitchen floor.
I wonder
about timing
a different clock, a different hour, a different day.
Sliding doors and missed chances.
What if it was yesterday?
Or tomorrow?
I wonder
about luck,

links in a chain,

dominoes,

a corner puzzle piece when you have two sides.

I wonder

When I finish the poem, I'm kneeling at the edge of the stage. The quiet escapes out the back while everyone in the first four rows stands. Cheering. Me. Molly. My insides do a victory dance. I bow and take my seat next to Hannah. A little hand squeeze. Bridgett goes next. Her obsession with obituaries is not left out of her poetry. Her words are sad and dark, but somehow she makes them sound like a beautiful song. I clap loudly. Hannah pretends she's busy with something else and can't applaud. She's not a fan. Of obituaries or Bridgett. And if I'm being totally honest, Bridgett kind of deserves that. Ever since they both showed up to Richie C.'s fifth-grade Halloween party wearing the same zombie bride costume, B has sort-of-kind-of not been so nice to Hannah.

Hannah's the last to go. She bows her head; the bangs hang like a slope in front of her face. Her poem is a tribute to Fred. I decide for her next birthday I'll get her a new Siamese fighting fish from Pete's Pet Palace.

When all the poets have spoken, Ms. P. steps onto the stage and says into the microphone, "I will make the announcement tomorrow as to which two classmates will move on to Round Two of the Poetry Slam Contest." Spit flies from her mouth and I'm thankful there are four rows between us. "Nice job today, everyone."

The bell sounds the end of the day, and I run home to tell Dad or Kate or Ian, but when I get there, the house is echo-empty. I take the stairs two steps at a time. In the mirror, I see my braces under my smile and I don't even care. I love today. I spin sixteen times and fall onto my bed, dizzy.

I exhale and open my eyes. I wait for the room to stop spinning. I grab four red Twizzlers, pop in my earbuds, and click on the B. B. King playlist I made during art on Monday. We're on the watercolors unit and I'm more of a stay-in-the-lines artist.

I skip to track four. This is Mom's favorite song. Ideas swirl in my head for my next poem. I need to move on to Round Two. Then the final round. Then I need to win. The whole thing. My plan depends on it.

This past Saturday, I came millimeters close to making a ginormous mistake that could have ruined my chances of winning the slam and my plan. I was shopping at

Shine Gifts and Gems with Hannah when I almost bought the glass giraffe. Its long sunflower neck and cocoa spots were a splash of yellow against the white shelf. It was so beautiful, but a possibly disastrous purchase just a few days before Round One. Thankfully, I realized that before the clerk with dirty fingernails rang up the sale. I didn't tell Hannah why I returned Sir Giraffe to his shelf, but if I had bought him, then my collection would have forty-five glass figurines. Forty-five—a terrible odd number. I decided to wait until I could buy Sir Giraffe *and* Monsieur Kangaroo.

I grab a ruler and lay it along my snowy white dresser to carefully align my glass zebra so it sits exactly one inch from the blue glass dolphin. I pick up the giant panda (an awesome birthday gift from Kate and Ian), set her down on her paws, slowly reach for the elephant, and rest it precisely one inch away. I finish with the stallion and cow. Finally, they're all perfectly aligned. I step back and exhale. So beautiful.

Except for the pink glass perfume bottle. It's lost next to the whale.

I pick up the perfume and roll it between my palms. Mom let me borrow it. Then she told me about the guy she sat next to on the T who pulled out an eight-inch hunk of cheddar and ate it like a Snickers. That was kind of our thing. Not the cheddar, but lying beside each other on my bed and sharing the weirdest thing that happened that day. Now every time I'm on the T, I look for the Cheese Man. No sightings yet.

The perfume smells like jasmine and mint. Mom said Dad had the scent made for her for their tenth anniversary. I spray my wrists with I Love You Forever and wonder if the bottle will last for the entire year.

Three hundred sixty-five days is a really long time.

2

the juice lady

NOW THAT ROUND ONE is over, I can get back to working on my class presentation for Ms. P. It's due tomorrow. The make-your-own-business project is supposed to include forty-five color-coded index cards, one poster, one five-minute oral presentation, and a six-page paper with a fancy see-through cover and bibliography. After Ryan Mantis wanted to create a business that sold air, Ms. P. suggested with her stern pay-attention voice that we choose our businesses wisely. I created Molly's Personal Organizing Service—Bringing Order to Disorder. I look over my checklist for tomorrow's presentation.

Knock, knock.

"Not sure why you bother knocking if you're just going to open the door and walk right in," I say.

Ian tilts his head. "Want to play with Spider?" He sticks his pygmy hedgehog in my face.

I shake my head. "No, I don't want to play with Spider." Not today.

Not ever.

Dad got it for him. He had said, "Your brother's having trouble sleeping, and hedgehogs are nocturnal. I think it will be good company."

Seemed a bit extreme. Owls are nocturnal, too, but he didn't get him one of those. I mean, the last time Ian's not sleeping landed him at the foot of my bed in his Spider-Man pajamas, I gave him my very non-living-non-nocturnal glass hippo, and he fell right asleep. Besides, it took Kate a year to convince Dad to get Oscar from the dog shelter, and he's a normal pet if you ignore his love of frozen peas.

Spider curls up into a spiky ball at the sound of my voice.

Ian pops next to me on my bed and tucks his little hand in mine. His smile shows off his missing front tooth. I'm happy the tooth fairy was around to see him lose his first tooth.

Mom's office closed at the end of school last year. Well, it wasn't exactly an office, more like a warehouse with a lot of blenders, veggies, and fruit. Mom's one of the Juice Ladies. When she got notice the business was shutting down, I have to confess that I was kind of relieved. She had spent the last five years inventing new ways to torture Ian, Kate, and me by squeezing the hearty, so-good-for-you juice out of every type of fruit and vegetable. I didn't even know kale and broccoli had juice.

I figured when the job ended, so would the swamp juice. But the company decided the States was not their target market after all, and they needed to send Mom to Canada for one year to launch their new juice line. Her choice—Toronto or unemployment. Mine—move to Toronto with Juice Lady or stay in Lantern, Massachusetts, with Dad. I chose to stay. Kate chose not to talk about it and Ian chose to do whatever I did.

Ian slips an almond out of his pocket for Spider. "I saw Hannah today. Her hair is blue."

"I know."

"Are you going to have blue hair?"

"Never. Why?"

"Just checking if that was something we were doing."

"What are we doing?" Kate asks from the doorway.

"Don't you knock?"

"We are *not* getting blue hair," Ian says as Spider crawls up his arm.

"Obviously," Kate says, running her hand through her black-as-night curls and scooping up Spider.

It's all so easy for her. She doesn't care that Spider's dirty and prickly and, well, dirty. "Hey, your poem rocked today," Kate says.

"Thanks, but how did you hear it? You're not even in the same school as me anymore." Kate's a freshman at Lakeville High.

"The high school had some half-day teacher workshop thing, so Kevin and I snuck into the back of the auditorium just in time to hear your slam."

I stare in disbelief as I watch her try to kiss Spider.

"Kevin and I think you could totally move on."

"Thanks." A bit awkward to think I was part of a conversation between Kate and her I-can't-live-for-thirty-seconds-without-him sophomore boyfriend.

"I liked the black cat part. I mean, I don't buy into the whole superstition thing. You totally rule your own destiny. Cat or no cat. But it sounded deep."

I nod, but don't hear a word she's saying. Spider has moved from kissing to climbing onto her shoulder and is heading down her back, toward my bed. No towel.

I'm trying to decide if it would be worse to catch him in my bare hands or have him land on my comforter when Ian grabs him. "I'm going to show Dad how Spider can sleep in his sock."

Before Kate or I can ask what he's talking about, he whips out one of Dad's long navy dress socks from his pocket, Spider crawls in, and they leave my room. Kate follows them.

My checklist for my business presentation is still on my bed, thankfully untouched by Spider.

Top of the list—*get shoe boxes*. First stop, Mom's closet.

I crack open the doors and slide onto the honey-colored wood floor. There are no clothes, no shoes, not even a belt left. I set my special sea glass down on the bare wood. Mom and I found it together on Chapin Beach when I was six. Two pieces had washed up on the sand next to each other. One turquoise and one gold. Mom kept the gold and I have the turquoise. It's always with me, so I never have to be without it *and* her.

Her clothes and shoes are gone, but the empty shoe boxes remain neatly stacked in the corner. A shiny red-checked box from the ballet flats I used to borrow, a long black box from the matching leather boots she bought for our birthdays last year, a white striped one from her fancy silver sandals she never wore, and the neon-orange box the running shoes came in when she decided she needed to start exercising. I like to sit in here. It smells like jasmine and mint and reminds me of her. My phone blasts the first twenty-four bars of Mom's favorite B. B. King song. I hit Ignore. It's just a reminder. Thirty-two days until Mom's first scheduled visit.

The door to the closet creaks open. Kate stands there staring at me. "What are you doing in here?"

"Nothing," I say. "What are *you* doing here?"

She slides next to me on the closet floor.

"Sometimes when I miss her most I come in here," she says.

I take her hand and we sit on the floor of Mom's closet together. Being next to her feels like a little slice of Mom is with me. Everyone always says she's the mirror image of Mom. The black curls, white-as-sand skin, and crystal-blue eyes. Kate tells me her favorite Mom things, which include almost everything but swamp juice and moving to Toronto.

"I miss her laugh," I say. It's from-her-belly loud and always lasts a beat longer than it should. Neither of us says anything for a while. Lost in our own Mom-moments.

That quiet ends when Ian and sock-Spider poke into the closet. "Can't find Dad. Have you seen him?"

We shake our heads no.

Ian stares at us. "Why are you guys sitting on the floor of Mom's closet?"

"Just talking," I say. He doesn't need to know that *we* miss Mom's laugh, her bad sense of direction, her lasagna. It's already too hard for him. It's been three weeks since she drove out of the driveway in the back of a cab and he still can't sleep at night.

"Sounds boring." He grabs sock-Spider and just before he leaves says, "The closet smells like her."

"I know," is all I say.

When he's gone, I ask Kate what's been swimming in my brain since Mom left. "Do you think she's ever coming back?"

She stares at me. "Pinky-swear honest?"

"Pinky-swear honest."

"No."

3

going is not the same as leaving

HER "NO" BOUNCES OFF the ceiling and smacks me in the face. I hear Mom's voice promising me she'll only be gone for one year.

"But she swore she was coming back. That this was temporary," I say.

"Like their separation?"

I ignore her. "She said that she was going *to* a job." I have the day she's coming back circled on my calendar. A year from the date she left.

She stops shaking her head and stares at me with that little-sister-you're-such-an-idiot look. I've seen it before. More than once. "Believe what you want."

"Mom told me that going to something was not the

same as leaving. She said there's a difference." I squeeze my sea glass.

Kate picks at the green polish on her nails. "I don't know why you keep defending her. I'm not the only one she left behind."

"She's coming back. She promised." I pause. Then, "Anyway, I have a plan."

Kate's right eyebrow arches. Another thing she got from Mom. "What kind of plan?"

"A plan to get her back here. For good."

"How?" Kate wants to know.

"I win the slam."

"Your big plan to get our mom to leave Canada and come home is to win a poetry competition at your middle school?" A smirk slips through.

"Look, the winner gets a big banquet in her honor with her whole family. They even get to sit at a special table with a white tablecloth. Mom would definitely come back for that. And once she's home, she'll remember how great it is to be together, how much she's missed us, and she'll stay." I stare at Kate, waiting for the smirk to morph into a congratulations-on-your-brilliant-plan smile.

It doesn't. Her lips flatten. "You're only making this

harder on yourself, Mol. If you, me, Ian, and Dad weren't enough for her *not* to leave, then a linen tablecloth and overcooked turkey at some stupid banquet aren't going to be enough to get her to come home."

My heart sinks into the floor of the empty closet, but I have to believe I can do this. I have to believe I can get her back.

"My plan will work," I argue.

"Honestly, Mol, neither your stupid sea glass nor your master plan will bring her home. She left us. On purpose. Deal with it," Kate says.

I notice her right ring finger no longer has even a trace of green polish. "You're wrong," I say. Then my mind goes to Ian. He's too young, too sweet, and too innocent to think Mom would just turn around and leave us. Forever. "Don't you dare tell Ian what you think about Mom."

She snorts. "You can't even say it. You can't even say that I think that Mom's never ever coming back."

I glare at her. "Just promise me that you won't say anything to Ian."

"Pinky swear."

Kate's phone rings "Paired" by the Penguins. "Kevin,

hold on," she says as she leaves the closet and runs into her room.

Now it's just me and the jasmine and mint. I sit for a while, thinking about pre-Toronto Mom. Kate's words creep into my brain. I stuff them somewhere down deep, grab as many boxes as I can carry, leave the closet, and head downstairs.

The cold air in the basement hits me on step eight. To the right on the wall are pictures of Kate, Ian, and me at our birthday parties. I stare at the one of Hannah and me eating chocolate cake at my tenth birthday party. Her hair is brown. No bangs. When Hannah walked in that day, she handed me a package wrapped in aluminum foil. A tinfoil ball really. Inside were two glass figurines—a cow and a piglet. She said since I had turned double digits I should get two. I loved my tenth birthday. Everything was perfect if you ignored the brownish-green swamp juice we had with my cake. I'd just turned ten, our whole house smelled like chocolate, and Mom and Dad made me a birthday scavenger hunt. That was long before their official temporary separation that started just six months before Mom fled to Toronto and our kitchen smelled like takeout all the time.

I spread a clean white sheet on top of the orange shag carpet and line up the boxes next to the files and the ziplock plastic bags. The antique mirror that Dad got to surprise Mom hangs to my right. Dad thought Mom would love it. She didn't. She thought it was just old. I stare into the mirror and decide to keep my hair exactly the same until she gets back. We got our hair cut together the week she left. She didn't even have an appointment. I did. But when Gwen-with-all-the-bird-tattoos finished trimming my hair, Mom whispered something to her. Forty minutes later, Mom's hair was five inches shorter.

She said she loved it. She needed a change. Something totally new.

I look in the mirror and measure from roots to ends. Twenty-six inches.

I get back to work. Next on my checklist, a sign. I grab some paper and the colored Sharpies (they don't smudge when you write) from the art corner of the basement. I leave the red glitter in the cabinet. With my ruler and stencils I write my business name across the top of the paper.

Molly's Personal Organizing Service—
Bringing Order to Disorder

Principles of Organizing

1. PICK UP
2. SORT AND FILE
3. LABEL
4. NO PAPER LEFT BEHIND

I hold up my new sign and stand in front of the mirror. I begin rehearsing my presentation when I notice the *B* in *LABEL* is crooked. I try to ignore it and continue, but I can't. I straighten my glasses, tighten my hair clip, and rip my paper into shreds.

4

boogies on the wall

BY THE TIME I finish everything for my presentation, it's way later than my Dad-approved bedtime.

I try to quietly sneak past Dad, who's still sitting in his big brown leather office chair at the computer, making his way through a family-size bag of sour-cream-and-onion chips.

"Honey, it's late and tomorrow's a school day," he says, his eyes glued on the papers spread across his desk.

So much for stealth mode.

"It's not so late. Bridgett never goes to bed before midnight."

Dad unsticks. "Well, last I checked, I'm not Bridgett's father."

Dad always says that stuff. *I don't care what other kids*

are doing. I'm not such and such's father. But then I spy the corners folded down in pages of his *Parenting* and *Raising Kids Today* magazines that I see every time I go into his office. Makes me think he kind of cares what other families are doing. But I know it's a useless argument. Especially at this hour. I kiss him good night.

On the way to my room, I hear, "*Psst. Psst. Psst,*" coming from Ian's room. When I poke my head in, Spider's staring at me from his cage and Ian's sitting up in his bed. "I can't sleep. Will you read to me?"

"Buddy, it's late."

He slides over and hands me *Goodnight Moon*, knowing I won't say no.

I straighten the tilted picture of both Spider-Man and Peter Parker on his wall, climb into bed beside him, and start to read. When I get to the end of the story, he says good night to Spider, the glass hippo I gave him, his favorite green shirt, the clown statue from Aunt Lucy, Spider-Man, and Peter Parker. I get up to leave.

He tugs on the sleeve of my shirt. "Will you stay with me for just a little bit more?"

I look over at Spider spinning to nowhere on his wheel. "Two minutes. Dad's already given me his Parenting 101 lecture on my need for sleep."

As I settle in again, I count eighteen little brown balls stuck to his superhero wallpaper. "Ian, what's all over your wall?"

He turns away.

"Buddy, what's all over your wall?"

"They're my boogies," he whispers.

I swallow the spit rising in my throat. There are so many things wrong with this.

I point to the tissue box on the shelf next to his bed. "You have tissues right here. Why are you putting your boogers on the wall?"

"They're too sticky."

"Ian, that's gross. I don't care how gooey they are. Anything that comes out of your nose goes into a tissue. Got it?"

He hides under his covers. "Are you mad at me?"

I lift the blanket and scoop him close. "No, just no more boogies on the wall."

I snuggle with him for a while, and when I think he's fallen asleep I slide off the bed and tiptoe to the door. Before I leave his room, I hear his small, tired voice say, "I love you, Molly."

"Love you, too, Buddy. Sweet dreams." He says he misses Mom most at bedtime. The other night I rolled over and found him curled up asleep in the middle of my floor. I laid my orange fuzzy blanket over him and whispered in his ear that everything was going to be okay.

I leave his door wide open. Another post-Mom-departure habit. Tiredness pours over my body. I flop onto my bed. Clothes on.

"Molly, why is your light still on?" Dad calls from downstairs.

How can he even see into my room? I pick up Daisy, the stuffed cow I got for my eighth birthday, and stare into her black, beady eyes. Then I stick out my tongue. I figure if Dad's planted some kind of spy camera, he'll have something to say about that.

No comment.

"I'm turning it off right now." Flick light switch off. Doesn't feel right. Flick it back on.

"Honey, what's going on in there?"

I pick up Daisy again. Turn her upside down to see if there are any wires or batteries hidden in her udders, but find nothing.

"Uh, I just forgot to put something in my bag for tomorrow."

Lie.

Dad comes upstairs and walks into my room. "Enough. It's bedtime. And it's late. Even for Bridgett." The bright red lights on my clock flash 12:10 a.m. Dad smiles, leans over, and kisses my forehead. His loose, hanging tie brushes my cheek. "You okay?"

"Mm-hmm."

"Then good night. And leave the light off."

I'll try.

"Night, Dad." He's gone. Relief. I grab my glasses, hop out of bed, and close my bedroom door. I use the flashlight I keep next to my bed to find my earbuds and my reggae playlist. By now I know it'll take at least three songs to finish my bedtime routine.

I want to rehearse my presentation before school. *But is my alarm on? I think so. I checked it. Maybe I'm wrong. I'll check it once more. Alarm's on. Perfect.*

I'm mesmerized by the rhythm of the music. When Dad comes back into the room, I'm organizing my socks in the glow of my flashlight.

"Molly."

He's standing at my door. I slowly slide my earbuds out one at a time.

"I was just—I was just—um. Looking for something," I manage to say as the lie unscrambles in my brain.

He sits on the edge of my bed and motions for me to get under the covers. My clock flashes 12:35 a.m. His tie's gone, replaced with a white T-shirt and his Middlebury College navy sweatpants. He's carrying his briefcase. Still working.

"Mol, you can't keep doing this."

I freeze and stare at him too long, but he doesn't continue. I exhale. "Well, you can't keep working all night." I glide into bed.

"Agreed. I will try if you will."

I nod. "I just need to recheck my alarm and then I'll really be ready." I start to fold back the comforter.

My dad pats my shoulder. "Stay in bed. It's so late already. I'll check your alarm. Good night, sweetheart," he says, closing the door behind him.

"Night, night, night, night," I say softly to the back of my door.

5

the remains of the
breakfast burrito

MY SHIRT'S IRONED, HAIR'S straightened, and supplies are ready to go. I put on my new glasses and stare in the mirror, hoping they look more newscaster than librarian. Then I check my list one more time to make sure I have everything I need for my presentation.

- *Principles of Organizing poster*
- *Index cards*
- *Six-page paper complete with fancy see-through cover*
- *Organizing supplies*
  - *Boxes*
  - *Sharpies*

- *Labels*
- *Files*
- *Baggies*
- *Colored pencils*

In the kitchen, Ian's making words with his alphabet cereal. Spelled out on the wooden table is: *MOM SPIDE* (no *R*) *MOLLY GOAT*. I stare at the words and hope goats aren't nocturnal. Dad may have to buy him one of those, too.

"Have a good day, Buddy," I say on my way out the door.

As I get to Mrs. Melvin's house, I see Hannah running toward me. Her black-and-blue pixie blows wildly in the cool September wind. Mrs. Melvin lives in the white ranch right smack between my house and Hannah's.

"Love the glasses," Hannah says as she catches her breath and wipes the sweat from her upper lip.

"Thanks. Do you think they look more librarian, scientist, or TV news anchor?"

Hannah stops, steps back, and takes a good look. Then she shrugs. "I don't know. They just look like glasses."

I grab her hand and give it a squeeze. "I'm so nervous about the poetry slam."

"Pretty sure I'm done, but you'll definitely move on. No one got more claps, cheers, and snaps than you. You've totally got this."

"You really think so? Honest, honest?"

She nods and crosses her heart, then sticks her wrist in my face. "Like them?"

Seven different braided bracelets cover her arm. I stare at the bracelets and wish she had made just one more.

"Braided bracelets. They are really popular in California. Each color strand has a different meaning. E. B. Rule Number 16: If you see a trend, embrace it."

Hannah lives by the book *E. B.'s Rules to Becoming a Successful Businesswoman.* A gift from her Dad after her first business, Lemonade on Laurel Lane, flopped. It was the start of last summer and we spent two hours making lemonade and waiting in the hot sun for the customers who never came. I washed my hands forty-four times that day. Forty-four. I don't know what was weirder: that I washed my hands so many times or that I counted. I remember standing at the sink in Hannah's kitchen.

Soap.

Water.

Rub.

Rinse.

The pink lemonade mix was sticky like syrup. Even when I saw the bubblegum shade of water disappear down the drain, I couldn't stop. The mix felt trapped in my skin. I told myself not to be so weird. It worked then.

Sort of.

Hannah's voice snaps me back. "So this is my business. Color Me Bracelets. What do you think?"

"I love it."

She smiles. "Now I need a favor. During my presentation, when Ms. P. asks for comments or questions, you have to raise your hand, say something positive, and place an order."

"Okay. Sure."

"It's important."

"Got it."

"Promise?" she asks.

"Promise. But first you have to get the cream cheese out from between your braces," I say.

Hannah swirls her tongue across her teeth and smiles big. "Is it gone?"

I nod.

It takes us just five more minutes to get to the bench outside of school. Hannah looks all serious. "I need to tell you something. It's big. Sit with me."

I stare at the bench. Peeling paint. Dried mustard. Dirt. I stuff my hands into my pockets and try a cleansing yoga breath, but my Zen moment sticks in my throat. "Um. I'm good here."

Hannah dumps her backpack next to her and I silently pray it doesn't land in the mustard. She leans in to tell me her news when Bridgett shows up.

"Richie Keegan threw up on the bus this morning," Bridgett says, completely ignoring Hannah.

Bridgett looks at me. "Why are you just standing out here?"

Before I can answer, she shrugs and continues. "First, I love the glasses. So totally country-singer star meets New Yorker."

"Thanks."

"Second, I'm freaking out about the slam. I need to know who's moving on. Third, and so much more criti-cal, did you see the obits today?"

How can she possibly think the obituaries are more important than the slam? The slam is everything.

"Page six, column three. Three paragraphs on the nineteen-year-old boy who died when he collapsed on the football field. Some undiagnosed heart thing. Page seven, half a page on Bart Linden, founder of some revolutionary microchip, who died at age seventy-two from a heart attack. Page six, column five, Gertrude Klein, eighty-six-year-old woman who died in her sleep. Two lines. She lived until eighty-six and only got two lines."

"So?" I stare at the remains of the breakfast burrito stuck to Bridgett's hands. I pull out my hand sanitizer and squirt some into her palms.

"You're so weird." She rubs her hands together. "Don't you see? We have to die young or famous for anyone to care enough to write about us when we leave this earth."

There's still cheese on her pinky.

The school bell rings. We grab our stuff and head into Room 820.

"I promise if you live a long life, but die before me, I'll write an obituary for you that will be at least half a page."

"Me, too?" Hannah chimes in.

I nod.

"It's not funny." Bridgett bites a hangnail off her thumb. "What if you die first?"

I smile. "Then you'll have no choice but to become famous."

6

wishing for
sandal season

MS. P. HOLDS TWO fingers in the air to signal us to stop talking. I know what's coming. Round One results. My insides swim like guppies.

"Class, all the students who participated in the Poetry Slam competition did an outstanding job. The two students from our class who will be moving on to Round Two are Josh and—"

Please let the next name be mine.

One last check of my colored pencils. Red. Orange. Yellow. Green. Blue. Indigo. Violet. Perfect.

"—Molly."

A real smile finds its way across my face while my insides do a happy dance. Like when Mom and I made chocolate chip–oatmeal cookies (no kale or swamp juice) and ate the entire batch before dinner.

The class applauds. Mac is high-fiving Josh, Hannah jumps up and gives me a hug while B says, "Way to go" from across the room. My guppies are now champion swimmers.

"Round Two will be held during the last period of the day on Friday. Molly and Josh will be competing against the winners of the other seventh-grade English classes." Ms. P. congratulates us and then begins discussing the format for our business presentations. I don't really listen. I hold tight to my happy feeling so it can't slip away.

Ever.

Bridgett goes first with her Never Too Soon Obituary Writing Service, and then Ryan introduces the class to his Revolutionary Foul-Shot Basketball System. I wish he'd worn matching socks or long pants.

And then it's my turn. I remind myself to refocus on the yahoo-you-are-moving-on-to-Round-Two moment and not on mismatched socks. Deep breath. I set Principles of Organizing on the lip of the whiteboard, stare at the neatly aligned books on the back shelf (thank you,

Ms. P.), and begin. The words pour out like a poem. When I reach the last syllable, I exhale and take my seat.

Hannah's presentation comes just after Mac's Car Wash Service. She prances to the front of the classroom to present her Color Me Bracelets business. Last night, she told me she was going to wear her ballet flats instead of her green high-top sneakers so she wouldn't worry about tripping on her shoelaces.

Hannah shows the class her bracelets. The color chart is behind her.

```
Red = Courage
Pink = Love
Brown = Earth
Orange = Curiosity
Gold = Wealth
Yellow = Happiness
Green = Life
Blue = Peace
Purple = Magic
White = Purity
Black = Death
Gray = Sadness
```

Her letters are crooked. I scan the class. Bridgett's trying to get Greg's attention, and Josh is doing something on his calculator.

"There's a color and bracelet for everyone," Hannah says in her best E. B. voice. I glance over at Gretta. She's drawing a picture of the blue jay sitting on the ledge outside our classroom window. Hannah clears her throat and I smile at her.

"I can weave a bracelet with up to five colors for only three dollars. Today, these bracelets sell in California for twenty-five dollars."

"What? That's a total rip-off!" Mac calls out.

"Mac, it's impolite to yell out," says Ms. P. "There will be time at the end for questions."

"While our assignment called only for a business plan, I'm actually starting this business today," Hannah continues.

Maybe this is what she wanted to tell me.

"And for a lot less than it costs in California. I'll be taking orders when we go outside for morning stretch. Thank you. Any questions or comments?"

Hannah looks straight at me. I'm supposed to place my order. Now. I've decided on blue. All blue. I start to raise my hand when I notice Greg's socks out of the corner of my eye. One is tall brown and the other is short gray. I scan the classroom from the knees down. Most kids' socks are all messed up. Mac's are half up and half down. Josh's are completely scrunched down. Hannah's don't even match. Thankfully, Bridgett wore black argyles pulled neatly up to her knees.

Other hands shoot into the air while I do a sock survey.

Bridgett's hand waves like there's someone she knows across a large, crowded room. Hannah calls on Gretta.

"That's a cool idea, Hannah."

"Thanks."

Bridgett's hand still dances in the air.

"Um—um, Greg."

"Yeah, do guys wear these things?"

"Sure."

"We have time for one more question or comment," Ms. P. says.

Raise your hand. Tell her you want a blue one. Think of something to say. But I can't. My mind crowds with socks. Out of the twenty-two kids in our class, only four (thankfully four) are wearing socks that match and are pulled up. I really need it to be the summer when everyone can just wear flip-flops.

Hannah calls on Bridgett reluctantly.

"This is, like, a total scam. It's not like I'm going to die if I wear a black one." She glances at Arianna, her shadow puppet, who robotically nods in agreement. "Hannah's like Lily P. Grant, the con artist who died Saturday at the age of sixty-three after scamming a bunch of old people out of thousands of dollars."

"That's enough, Bridgett," Ms. P. says.

"It's not my fault; it's the truth. You can read it for yourself in section C, page four of the obituaries in today's *Boston Globe*."

Ms. P. ignores Bridgett. "Well done, Hannah. Very unique."

Hannah grins and shows off her red-and-orange braces.

I give her a thumbs-up as she takes her seat, and slip her a note that says I want a blue one.

She crumples the note.

7

the opposite of pod

"WAIT UP," I CALL to Hannah on the way out to morning stretch. Kate said they stopped calling it recess in middle school to make us feel like we weren't elementary school babies anymore.

She stops. "What?"

"I love the bracelets. You did a great job. I so want one!"

Eye roll. "You broke your promise. You told me you'd raise your hand and order one when Ms. P. called for comments or questions."

I bite the inside of my mouth hard. I taste the warm blood trickling down my throat.

Silence.

Hannah knows me better than anyone. She knows

I slept with my closet light on until fifth grade and that I'm afraid of cats, particularly those white ones with the red eyes. I can't pretend with her. "I'm sorry. I definitely want a blue one and promise to wear it every day. I just got, um, distracted." That's as honest as I can be.

"By what?" she asks.

"What *what*?"

"What was so distracting?"

Socks. I can't say that. "Just something dumb." I know it's a pathetic answer, but it's the only one I can give.

"So, you ignored my presentation because you were thinking about *something dumb*."

My brain searches frantically for a better lie. "I um, um, was worried about Round Two of the slam. I don't even have the shred of an idea for my poem, and I bet Josh's already written his."

She stares into my eyes. I hope she can't see me. The real me. "I don't care what Josh Finnegan does, there's no way he's going to beat you. Besides, the kid never blinks and barely speaks. I think he's part stone," she says, her anger slipping away.

A smile finds my face. Then, "I'm sorry. Don't be mad." I look at the sandy ground.

"I'm not mad. I just didn't want to have to call on Bridgett."

"She's harmless." Mostly because all she cares about is herself.

"She's obsessed with dead people and hates me," Hannah says.

"She *is* obsessed with dead people, but she doesn't hate you. She just doesn't know you the way I do."

Hannah twirls her too-short hair tightly around her finger until the tip turns reddish blue.

"Okay, out with it," I say.

"What?"

"What's wrong? You only do that hair thing when you're upset. And your hair isn't even long enough now to do it properly." I unwrap her finger.

"This was the thing I wanted to tell you this morning before Ms. Death showed up. This is a double-cross-your-heart-swear-not-to-share secret," she whispers.

I swear and we seal it with our pinky shake.

"Okay, when my dad thought I was asleep on the couch, I overheard him talking to my gram on the phone. You know he was laid off, right?"

I nod. Hannah's dad was the chef at Bayside Bistro until they fired him for some fancy French chef named

Pierre. I figured by now things were fine. I mean, it wasn't like her dad moved away from her family to make swamp juice in Canada.

"He said that money's tight and it's getting harder to find another job around here, and then he mentioned a job offer in Seattle."

I stare at her to see if there's a just-joking behind her story, but there isn't. "Seattle? Your dad's going to Seattle?"

"No. He's not going to Seattle *without me*."

"I didn't mean he'd leave you alone. Can't you stay with your gram?" It's been just Hannah and her dad since her mom died a gazillion years ago when Hannah was little.

"No, he says we're a pod. If he goes, I go."

I guess my family isn't a pod. I wonder what the opposite of a pod is.

Hannah continues, "Except clearly we're not a pod since we live on land and despite the larger-than-average size of the Levine butts, we're not whales."

I'm stuck on the leaving part. "Hannah, you can't go. Seattle's so far, it's a whole different time zone!"

"I know."

"And I'd miss you, and my missing-bucket is already full with my mom."

"I know," she says again, grabbing a blue strand and going for another twirl.

"So what did he say next?"

"I don't know. I woke up from my pretend sleep because I couldn't listen to him for one more second."

"What? Why? Didn't you want to hear the rest?" I notice her seven bracelets. Green. Orange. Red. Yellow. Purple and white. Pink and gold. And the last one is a mix of all the colors. No pattern. Deep breath.

Hannah stares at the ground. "I did, but I freaked out. What if I have to move?" The twirl is turning her finger the color of her hair.

I unwind her hair again. "Fine. Even if you do leave me, which you won't, we'll talk every night like I do with my mom. Plus, we'll spend all our vacations and summers together." I hug her tight.

"It's not the same. Seattle's all the way across the country. It rains there and I already have terrible hair," Hannah says.

"You don't have terrible hair. It's just short and black and blue and uneven."

"What am I going to do? I don't want to move." Hannah rests her head on my shoulder.

"Don't worry, we'll think of something." I lean my head into hers. "I promise."

As we walk together around the empty rock garden, Hannah says, "I've already decided that I'll give my dad the money I make from the Color Me Bracelets business. Maybe it can help. Even a little."

"So that's why you're doing the business for real?"

She nods.

"But no matter what business I create, unless I come up with some incredible phone app—and that's unlikely since I don't know anything about computer programming, I hate science, and I'm very average in math—it's not going to change anything."

We are quiet for a while.

Then I say, "Hey, do you remember when Kayla from camp won five thousand dollars in that Next Great Diva singing contest?"

"That's not even a little funny. You know I sound like a dying cat when I sing the 'Star-Spangled Banner.' Don't think a singing contest is an option."

"I know you can't sing. No offense—"

"None taken."

"But there have to be other contests."

Hannah stops walking and looks me square in the eyes. "You really are a genius." Then she hugs me tight. When we were little we had hugging contests to see how long we could walk, eat, and play while hugging. Usually, after about ten minutes, one of us had to pee. We would fall down, untangle our arms, and giggle until we got all serious and tried again. Today, we hold on tighter than usual and there's no giggle.

We only let go when Gretta calls Hannah over to buy a yellow-and-orange bracelet.

I watch the back of Hannah's navy sweater march off toward her. A group of kids plays kickball in the field. Bridgett and Arianna opt out and huddle near the bleachers. They wave me to join them. I nod like I'll be there when I'm free.

The duo thinks I'm like them. They don't know that Perfect Molly is a fake. They don't know that she doesn't even exist. I start to walk over to them and then look down. The rocks aren't quite aligned. Not now. Keep walking. I look down again. Still crooked. I look around.

No one's paying attention to me. Let me just move this dusty beige one a little back and this brown one forward a pinch. There, that's better. I stand up and brush the gravel from my hands.

I gaze proudly at my neat line of stones.

8

rules of *roygbiv*

THE BELL RINGS AND morning stretch is over. Hannah finds me. She loops her arm in mine and we head back into the classroom. She's telling me about all the bracelet sales she just made when Greg flies into my desk and all of my newly sharpened pencils, clean erasers, highlighters in every color, Sharpies that don't smudge, and colored pencils scatter onto the floor. My papers go everywhere. *No!*

Greg stumbles as he gets up, tossing the football he just caught back over to Josh.

"Oops. Sorry 'bout that," Greg says.

Sorry. Really? Now I have to reorganize everything.

I turn to Greg and with my biggest grin, I say, "It's cool. No big deal."

The lie flows out of my mouth so easily. A big fat lie. It's me talking, but the other me. The one who kids like. The one who isn't crazy.

"Greg and Josh, you'll be inside for morning stretch tomorrow. You know the rules. No throwing balls inside the school building." Ms. P. stands statue-still at the front of the class.

Greg looks my way, mouths "sorry" again, and then smiles, showing off his navy-blue braces that are now filled with Oreo bits.

Gross.

I look over at Josh. No apology.

"Class, let's get started with English. In your reading last night from *Tuck Everlasting*, who can tell me why Winnie feels reassured when she hears the music box?"

Arianna's hand shoots up.

I know this, but I can't answer. Thanks to Josh and Greg, I'm now on the floor picking up my stuff.

"Want some help?"

I look up. Hannah's gathering my colored pencils.

She's doing it all wrong.

"Thanks, but I'm okay," I say.

You can't put the orange next to the black. It has to go

between the red and the yellow. ROYGBIV, the colors of the rainbow. Red. Orange. Yellow. Green. Blue. Indigo. Violet. That is the proper order.

Hannah has never understood that. Even when we were little, her box of crayons had the fire-engine red shoved next to the spring-grass green, the what-dreams-are-made-of black upside down against the broken, happy-face yellow.

My stomach is tight like a double knot. Deep breath. I'll fix it later.

"I got it. Really." My gritted teeth are making my jaw throb.

Ignoring me, Hannah picks up the papers strewn around my desk and says softly, "Greg and Josh are so stupid."

Some sheets are upside down, others sideways—none in date order. She goes on about the boys, but I stop listening. I grab a handful of papers. September 9, September 4, September 13. *Ugh! This is going to take forever. Look at this one. Poor September 5—not only is it turned upside down and backward, but it's wet and smudged.*

Ms. P. looks over. "Girls, wrap it up. It shouldn't take the entire lesson to clean up Molly's desk."

"Yes, Ms. Piper," Hannah and I say in unison.

I feel awful that I'm relieved when Hannah returns to her desk and thankful she doesn't notice. I can clean up this mess on my own. I dump the colored pencils into my lap.

ROYGBIV.

9

bargus clan
and the bug jar

LAST PERIOD OF THE day turns into a free study hall when Mr. Lampert, our History Through the Ages teacher, goes home with the flu.

Hannah slides her chair next to mine and opens her laptop. "Let's do a search for other contests."

Ten of the fifty search results come up. Hannah mutters as she scrolls down the list, "Design Your Own Cereal Box. No. Greeting Card. No. Paper Airplane. No. Website. No."

I notice the torn papers sticking out of her backpack and zip her bag closed.

Finally she says, "This is it!" She clicks the link to the Want to be a Teen Mogul website and reads, "Calling all teen entrepreneurs! Make money and create your own online business. It's simple. Come up with a fantastic idea. Submit your business plan here. A panel of business-people, along with five former contest winners, will judge each submission. If yours is selected, you'll win five thousand dollars and the support you'll need to make your business an online reality. Ages twelve to six-teen by September first eligible to enter. Contest opens September fifteenth."

"Hannah, this is perfect. You can totally do this," I say, giving Hannah's hand a gentle squeeze. Even though I know in the pit-of-my-stomach-where-the-truth-sits that no amount of contest or bracelet money will likely pre-vent her from moving, I also know if there was a contest I could have entered that might have made it a speck harder for my mom to leave, I would have entered it, too.

Hannah works on the application and I work on my next slam poem. I have to get it right, but it doesn't flow. The words tangle and stick. I put the not-close-to-finished poem away and pull out my red leather journal. The last joint Mom-and-Dad gift before their solo parent per-formances. Only a few empty pages left to fill with Me-poems.

These are safe.

Hidden.

Not to share. Not to slam.

I sharpen a new No. 2 and write:

Words scramble
Words slide
Feeling lost
Want to hide

Colors blend
Colors part
Feeling scared
In my heart

Before I can finish, Hannah hands me a piece of torn paper.

"I wrote down the things I need to do to enter. Will you help me answer these questions?" she asks.

"Sure." I tuck my journal back into my backpack.

Dog doodles decorate the entire left side of Hannah's paper, and the to-do's are less list and more random words scattered across the sheet.

I hand her back her paper and reach for her laptop. "Why don't you read me each step and I'll type it onto a fresh document."

It takes a few tries for her to read her own writing, but finally we make a list.

<u>Hannah's Teen Mogul Application To-Do List:</u>

1. Write business plan.
2. Take a picture of Hannah, making sure to highlight the blue tips and the uneven fringe bangs (Hannah added this last part.)
3. Answer the questions on the application:
   - Why do you want to start this business?
   - How did you come up with your business idea?
   - How much money do you anticipate needing to fund your business?
   - By what means will you let people know about your business?
   - Have you implemented your business yet? If so, how successful have you been?

- What are your plans for the money you earn?
4. Come up with the $35 contest entrance fee.

"Thirty-five dollars. How am I going to come up with that money?" Hannah asks as she tears off a corner of the paper and sticks her raspberry gum in the center.

I try hard to ignore the ripped paper and the wad of chewed gum. "I saw you talking to Gretta and Greg outside this afternoon. Did you make any sales?"

"Some." Hannah pulls a bug jar out of her bag and then navigates around the bug guts to grab the coins and dollars stuck to the bottom.

"You know, they've invented these amazing new gadgets called wallets," I say, cringing.

"Very funny. Look, if your little brother understood the concept of a short-term habitat, I wouldn't have to worry about beetle guts in my jar."

Point taken. Ian had borrowed Hannah's bug jar on Sunday when he collected a family of beetles. I guess the Bargus clan didn't fare well.

I hand her a clean ziplock baggie from my backpack.

"Thanks." She counts her money. "I have six dollars and fifty cents. Not exactly thirty-five dollars."

"You'll sell more bracelets. I know it! You said the business was hot."

She nodded.

"And once you get the money, we can ask Kate to use her credit card." Kate's the only non-grownup I know with a Visa card. Dad gave her the you-need-to-learn-responsible-spending speech and promptly got her a credit card with her name on it. One of the few Dad-speeches with a perk.

Hannah dumps her money into the ziplock baggie, tosses it into the bottom of her backpack, and opens her notebook on the desk. Scrawled all over the pages, in no particular order, are her favorite Rules to Becoming a Successful Businesswoman by E. B.

E. B. Rule No. 3: Always have a plan.

E. B. Rule No. 8: Be prepared.

E. B. Rule No. 15: Market. Market. Market.

E. B. Rule No. 9: Every business needs a set of rules.

E. B. Rule No. 18: Don't promise what you can't deliver.

E. B. Rule No. 2: Be confident.

E. B. Rule No. 11: Don't let people know what you're thinking.

E. B. Rule No. 13: Revel in your success.

E. B. Rule No. 4: Be flexible.

E. B. Rule No. 14: Have a designated work space.

E. B. Rule No. 1: Trust.

E. B. Rule No. 16: If you see a trend, embrace it.

E. B. Rule No. 7: Understand the big picture.

The spit rises in the back of my throat. *Why is number one near the bottom and fifteen near the top? Where are numbers five, six, ten, twelve, seventeen, nineteen, and twenty? I can understand not having five, but why seven and not six?* The disorder floods my brain. I look over at Hannah. She's happily chewing on a new piece of gum while typing up her business plan based on the mixed-up rules of Emma Brown. Emma Brown, or E. B., was on the cover of *Forbes* at the age of twenty-two. She had created some interactive site for teens and kids that sold for millions. She's Hannah's role model. For everything.

Amazingly, Hannah doesn't care that the rules are out of order.

I wish I didn't care.

10

worst word in *merriam-webster's dictionary*

SCHOOL ENDS. HANNAH SLAMS her locker closed and walks away. The door springs open again. I run back to close it.

I hurry to catch up to Hannah. "Hold on." Hannah stops walking.

"Here." I squirt hand sanitizer into her palms.

"What's this for?"

"Gretta told me that Mac went home sick. Mr. Lampert's sick and that kid on Bridgett's bus threw up this morning."

Hannah rubs her hands together and then flaps them around to air-dry.

I squeeze another round of germ-killing disinfectant into her hands. "Just to be safe."

She stares at me hard so no lies can slide out. "You all right?"

I look at my shoes. "I'm fine."

There goes one lie. *Fine.* The worst word in *Merriam-Webster's Dictionary.* I'm convinced the word *fine* means nothing good. It actually means nothing at all.

I hook my arm with hers and reroute the topic. "Let's go to Indulge. Dad said I could take the T if we go together."

Two sentences. No lies.

She gives me a smile full of braces. "Okay, but this time I'm only getting the sour apple, orange, and lemon jelly beans. Last time, the peach and watermelon made me sick."

Indulge is my favorite candy store, *and* it's Dad-approved since it's not far from the train station. I text Dad the plan. That's our deal. I get freedom as long as he's informed of my every movement. Our arrangement screams *Ask Maggie*'s back-to-school article in the September issue of *Parenting* magazine. The walk to the T is quick. Up Baldwin Street and down Lantern Lane. The Green Line feels surprisingly crowded for a Wednesday afternoon. I assumed everyone would already be where they needed to go by now. We move through a few sections of the train and finally find separate seats near the back. I take the one without stains, but decide to sit on my jacket anyway. The man next to me smells like rotten eggs. I try breathing through my mouth, but after two stops, I forget and take a big breath in. *Gross*. Thankfully, Egg Man gets off at Pear Crossing. Before Hannah can move over, another man sits down next to me, takes out a block of cheddar, and starts eating the brick. I can't believe it.

It's Cheese Man.

Hannah and I start to crack up. I text Mom.

We get off at the next stop and I check my phone. Nothing from Mom. I know she's probably selling her Beet-Kale-Pumpkin blend someplace where there's no reception, but I get a tug of worry that she's forgotten about me. I tuck my fear into my back right pocket. Mom says that's what you do with worries that you can't get rid of and can't control.

Indulge smells like the perfect blend of chocolate and sugar. Hannah fills her bag with jelly beans. "You know, staring at your phone isn't going to make her text you back. I'm sure she's just busy with all her juice stuff."

"I know." I put my phone away and get Twizzlers for me, gummy frogs for Ian, and Skittles for Dad. Kate's on a no-sugar thing.

No sign of Cheese Man on the return trip. "Let's drop the candy off for your dad and Ian, and then we can walk to my house to work on my application. I still need help with a few of the questions and the photo." Hannah shoves a handful of lemon jelly beans into her mouth at once and then makes a scrunched-up sour face.

"I have some stuff to do for my dad. So you head home and I'll come over to help as soon as I'm done."

"What do you have to do?"

"My dad told me I had to straighten my room and finish my chores as soon as I got home today. I left it sort of a mess this morning."

Not true.

"I also need to write and practice my new slam poem," I continue.

"Okay. Got it. New better plan," Hannah says, her hands dancing in the air. "Let's stop by your house first. I can help you finish your chores. I can even be your practice audience for your poem. Then—this is the genius part—we can grab something from your closet for me to wear for my photo shoot."

I nod. She's definitely going to need to borrow clothes that aren't brown, beige, or tan for the shoot.

Hannah's still talking. "After that, we can head to my

house together and work on the contest application. Besides, my dad invited you guys over for dinner. He's making his famous chicken parm with garlic bread."

"Cool. Great idea about the clothes. I'll ask my dad about dinner, but the other stuff, I can just do super fast myself, then meet you."

"You promise to pick out something good and be quick?"

"I promise."

Behind my back my fingers are crossed.

11

bad things will happen

WHEN I WALK INTO the house, I come inches from tripping over a gift from the Juice Lady. A case of the fall special—Kale, Carrots, Apples, and Harvest Spices—is sitting on the floor directly in front of the mudroom door. I check my phone. No new messages. I step over the case and go upstairs. I'm surprised to see Dad's navy suit jacket dangling over the kitchen chair.

"Dad?"

"In here," he yells from the home office he lives in when he's not working in Boston.

I poke my head in. Yesterday's *Boston Globe* sports section is on the floor, along with an empty bag of pretzels and a container of chocolate-covered almonds. His eyes are stuck on his computer, and he's running his hands through his recently grown goatee. "Why is there a case of juice downstairs and why are you home?" He usually makes an appearance closer to six, when Ian's afterschool day care ends.

He takes off his Red Sox cap to scratch his head. "The case is compliments of your mother."

I don't want her juice. I just want *her*. Home.

"And I got a call from Mrs. Washington that Ian was sick."

Mrs. Washington is Ian's teacher. I freeze and try to remember if I realigned all my colored pencils.

"Is he okay?" I ask.

Dad types something.

I cough to remind him I'm standing in the doorway. "Dad, what's wrong with Ian?" I have to know. It's *my* job to take care of him now. Mom's in Toronto. Dad's on deadline all the time. Kate's got more post-school work hours at Belts, Bags, and Bangles.

"He's just got a bad cold."

I exhale.

Dad then goes for the obligatory "How was your day?" but his eyes never move from the screen. "Shoot. I can't believe this guy."

"Day was fine. I made it to Round Two of the Poetry

Slam Contest. My presentation went well. But then this one boy—"

"Oh, before you go into your room, I need to prepare you. Ian got into your glass collection. I got him out before he did any real damage."

My worry changes to anger. "What?! You have to be kidding. First, the jerks at school knock over my desk and now my brother messes up my stuff!"

My head feels like there's hot metal swirling around.

"Sweetheart, it's really no big deal. He's little and was just playing."

No big deal.

"My door was shut. Who let him into my room?"

"No one. He must have gotten in while I was on a conference call for work. I'm sorry. I really am." His eyes momentarily unglue from the computer screen. "I was going to clean it up myself, but then got swamped with an article I need to finish for tomorrow. I'll come help you as soon as I finish this one thing."

Pause. Deep breath.

"Molly, I truly am sorry. I was in a bind. Ian was home sick and I did the best I could."

"This is all your fault! Ian. Mom. All of it!"

"Molly, that's not fair."

I toss the Skittles on his desk, drag my backpack up the stairs, and slowly crack open the door to my room, afraid to see what *no big deal* looks like. The giraffe is on the floor. Knocked over in a pile with the gorilla, lemur, bald eagle, and African elephant. I open the door a little farther. The rabbit, cow, and horse are facedown, grazing on my orange carpet. The panda, sheep, goat, ibex, skunk, wolf, dolphin, starfish, hippopotamus, cheetah, spider monkey, donkey, piglet, lion, tiger, brown bear, and bobcat are like my papers that Josh and Greg knocked over today—scattered about in no order. No order. *No big deal. Is he for real?*

The fox is lying on its side on my nightstand with Huey the raccoon.

My collection started with Huey. He was from Nana Rose. I sat next to Papa Lou, my grandpa, on a counter stool in the Rockville Diner for our special Sunday lunch, just the two of us. After our piled-high corned beef sandwich with Russian dressing and extra pickles, french fries, and chocolate milkshakes, he slid this beautiful animal out of his wool coat pocket and placed him in front of me. He told me the raccoon had been Nana

Rose's and she always wanted me to have it. "Find the perfect spot for him, Molly." Papa died two months later. Ian says he went to heaven to find Nana Rose.

My phone blasts B. B. King. It's my daily reminder— thirty-one days until Mom's visit. Unless my plan works. Then it could be as soon as the end of next week, when the winner of the slam is honored at the banquet. It's not just some dinner with school turkey and hot dogs. Kate's wrong. It's a big deal. There will be fancy tablecloths and waiters, and the *Boston Globe* always interviews the winner's family for the G section of the paper. Mom will love it.

I turn on some music and sit in the middle of my floor, hoping it will swallow me. I take off my glasses and spin them around eight times and pray I can find a way for this to feel like *no big deal.* I see the chimpanzee on its side. In my heart, I want to leave this mess and go to Hannah's. Last year, I could've left. I would have picked up my animals, put them back in their places, and been on my way. But now it takes so long to feel right.

I slide my glasses back on and separate the glass figures by habitat and color. Then I reach for my wooden ruler. There's a light tap on my door. Dad pokes his head in before I can tell him to leave me alone.

"Hey." He surveys the room and then me and my ruler. "I'm sorry. I know this is hard."

He sits next to me. A drop of sadness finds me.

"This isn't how I want things either." He lays his calloused hand on top of mine. "But it's no one's fault. It just is."

I bite my lip on the inside so he can't see.

"Look, I know I'm not always so good at this, but I'm working on it. I promise."

He starts to hum to the music. I used to love when he hummed. Now it just reminds me of what used to be. "Want one?" He holds out a palm of all different colored candies.

I take two green and two yellow.

"Hey, glad your presentation went well today." A warm smile spreads across his face.

I can't meet him in that happy place. My smile has slipped away. "I still have a lot to do."

"Want help?" He reaches for the rabbit.

"No, thanks."

"Very proud of you for making it to the next round in the slam contest," he says as he leaves my room.

I realize when he's back downstairs that I forgot to ask him about dinner at Hannah's. I'm sure he'll be working anyway. I spray my neck with Mom's perfume, pick up the cheetah, and begin aligning the animals again. One inch between figures. Next, the elephant. Then, the monkeys. Two kinds—gorilla and spider monkey. *Nope. The spider guy needs to slide back. It's too close to the wall behind it. A little farther. Back a bit. Up. Back. I hate this. I could be at Hannah's now. Good. Pause. Not good. Bring the gorilla up, too. All right, that's better. Feels right. Now for the farm animals. Cow.*

The buzz from my cell phone jars me.

Uh-oh.

"You said you'd be super quick and come right over," Hannah says.

I envision her standing with her hands on her hips.

"Where are you?"

"Home," I say.

"Still?"

"Yes. My dad was busy working. No surprise. And Ian got into my glass animals."

"And?"

"And that's it. I had to clean them up. You should have seen them. I haven't even gotten to finish my poem yet."

"Mol, you promised."

"I know. I'm really sorry," I mutter, desperate to share what I can't say aloud. *If things aren't in order, then I don't feel right. I have to find the right balance. Otherwise, everything will tip.*

Out.

Of.

Control.

"You totally blew me off. You said you would do your stuff and then bring the clothes and come over."

"I didn't realize that so much time had passed."

"What were you doing?" Pause. "Really."

"I told you. Cleaning."

Please don't make me explain. Please believe me.

"No one takes that long to clean up her stuff."

Silence. Thick as sludge.

"Look, I'm sorry. I have only a few more to put away, then I'll work on my poem just a little and come right over."

I promise.

I don't say that part out loud.

More silence on the other end. Hannah had hung up.

The horse is still nose-first in the carpet and the lion's more than an inch away from the giraffe, which means I have to realign each animal from the lion back.

Just stop.

I can't.

Why not?

If I don't do it right—if they're not aligned perfectly, then . . .

Then what? I yell at myself.

Bad things will happen.

To Ian.

What bad things? The sane part of me wants to know.

The mixed-up part of me doesn't answer.

12

cheese man sighting

MY PHONE RINGS AGAIN. I think it's Hannah calling back, but it's Mom.

"How's my girl? Did you get the juice?" she wants to know.

"Got the juice. And I'm fine." I rub the sea glass and try not to think about what Kate said. Mom wouldn't stay in Toronto. She wouldn't break her promise to come back in a year.

"You don't sound fine." Mom always knows. Maybe it's better she lives so far away and can't see the real me. But then I have to live with the empty hole in my stomach from all the missing.

I tell her about the poetry slam and let her flood the

phone with *ooh*s and *ahh*s and *I'm-so-proud-happy-excited*s.

"Weirdest thing that happened to you today?" she asks.

"Did you get my text? I saw Cheese Man."

"I did." I hear her laugh. The sound of it used to make me feel like nothing bad could ever really happen. Now it just reminds me of what's missing. "I meant to text you back, but was stuck in a juice convention. So, you met Mr. Cheddar. That totally qualifies as weird."

I lie down on my bed, look up at my ceiling, and imagine she's lying next to me.

"What about you?"

"You ready for this one? I walked into a bathroom at the convention and turned to the woman waiting at the door and said, 'Oh, when are you due?' And she said, 'I had my baby four months ago.'"

"No way." Despite myself, I laugh.

She laughs, too. It was like the time we took care of Aunt Lucy's parrot, Bertie. Mom tore open the bag of bird food and it spilled all over the floor. Mom shouted a very un-mom-like word that Bertie began to repeat. Over and over and over again. We laughed for the next hour as we swept up the bird food and listened to Bertie chant the very un-mom-like word.

It feels good to hear her voice. I miss it. I miss her. We talk for a while longer. She tells me about Toronto and the Canadian juice market.

Then she says, "Your room's ready whenever you want to visit."

"Thanks," is all I say. Kate already told me she's never going to Toronto, and Ian says he'll only go with me.

An awkward pause floats between us.

"I know it's a big trip. Just missing you. That's all."

"Miss you, too. But even if I don't make it to Toronto, you'll be back in thirty-one days," I remind her. Or hopefully earlier if my plan works.

She's silent.

"Right?"

Nothing.

"That's the date you told me that you were coming back to visit. Remember? It was right before you went to the airport."

"I remember. Mol, things are complicated."

"What's so complicated about getting on a plane and coming home when you promised to come home?"

"I gave you that date before I officially started working. I was hopeful, but it's a new job. I'm not sure I can leave when I want to."

I say nothing. My words are stolen by the breath leaking out of my lungs.

"I'll try. I promise," Mom says. "And even if I can't come back on that day, we'll pick a new date."

Silence.

"I love you very much," she says.

Then her voice disappears and the silence tugs at me. The missing feels bigger than my whole body. I need her to come back, and I believe in the pit-of-my-heart-where-I-miss-her-most that the only way to make sure that happens is to win the slam. Once she's at the slam banquet with Ian, Kate, Dad, and me, she'll remember how great it is to be together, how much she's missed us, and she won't want to leave. Not again. I grab my red leather journal, sharpen a new No. 2 with an untouched pink eraser, and write:

Catch me please, I'm falling fast
Can I come back or will this last?

As time slips, it's hard to hide
To keep my crazy tucked inside.

Peeks through cracks, to show its face
Why can't it just stay in one place?

I wonder if this is what it feels like to free-fall. My stomach grumbles. I look up. It's 6:30 p.m. We're usually eating dinner by now. I stay in my room until I finish aligning each animal and then step back to admire my work. Beautiful. The stiffness in my neck melts. The worry retracts.

The pounding fear that bad things will happen to Ian is new, though. When I can't find perfect, my mind spins with thoughts that he's alone and sick or hurt or worse— even if I know he's building a Lego castle in the room next to mine.

I put my journal away, step out of my room, but still no sign of dinner from Dad. Hannah's dad is a great cook. I wish we were eating dinner over there. Our house just smells like take-out pizza, Chinese food, or cleaning supplies all the time. No smell of Mom's peanut butter–chocolate chip cookies or her homemade cinnamon applesauce with the lumps still in it. No pans banging about in the kitchen.

"Dad," I call.

No answer.

"Dad!" I say a bit louder.

Nothing.

I march down the stairs. Through the window I see

the orange glow of the setting sun. Ian is on the couch watching cartoons. *Do not even think about talking to me, Mr. Destroyer.* I peek into the kitchen. The table is bare and the counters are clean.

The door to Dad's office is slightly ajar. He's still sitting at his computer, absorbed by a message flashing on the screen.

"Dad!"

"What?" he asks. "Why are you yelling?"

"I've called you four times."

"Sorry, honey. I'm just so busy right now." He spins around to look at me. "What's up?"

"It's late. Dinner. Remember?" I say in an attempt to jolt him back to parenthood.

"Oh, I didn't realize the time. Kate called and she's working tonight, so it's just Ian and you."

"Aren't you going to eat?" When Mom and Dad were Mom *and* Dad, he'd skip meals for a deadline, but that still left one parent sitting at the dinner table.

"Not now. I'll join you when I'm done. I have to finish this article for tomorrow. It's about the recession's impact on consumers' decisions to purchase safety equipment."

"Fascinating."

I wait to see if he's done. Then, "Can we eat now?"

"Oh, right."

He leaves the office and when he returns says, "Ian's feeling a little better and wants pizza. Since it's just you two, we can call Deno's and have them send over a cheese pizza."

"We?"

"Well, can you actually call since I've still got at least one more round of edits?"

It isn't his fault, really. Dad's just doing what he has to do to take care of us. And I guess so is Mom. If she hadn't taken the job in Canada, her company would have dumped her. Some days I miss Mom huge and other days it feels like I'm used to not having her around. I'm not sure which is worse.

The kitchen seems sterile. I think back to last Thanksgiving, when the kitchen smelled like turkey, stuffing, and apple crisp. Mom was still living in the same house and country. That was the last time I remember the kitchen smelling like something other than cleaning solution or takeout.

I open the drawer stuffed with menus. Disorder screams out. I dump the menus on the counter and organize them alphabetically. Deno's ends up on top. I grab the phone and dial. It's going to be an hour. As I hang up, I stare at the telephone number again. All odd numbers. No pattern. Figures.

Odd.

Just like me.

13

regular mad or slam-the-door-and-walk-away mad

I RING HANNAH'S DOORBELL and hold my breath. I don't know if she's regular mad or slam-the-door-and-walk-away mad.

She answers. "What?"

"Look, I'm really sorry."

Nothing.

I take it as a good sign and continue. "I have some time before I have to be back to feed Ian and figured we could work on your application." Awkward pause. "Can I come in?"

Hannah stands there for a long minute and then slides to the right. "Fine, but first I need to make some bracelets."

As we head out to the garage, Hannah's dad is hunkered over the stove stirring something.

"Hi, Molly," he says. His *Dads Make the Best Cooks* apron drapes over his round belly, protecting his tan pants from the spray of tomato sauce.

"Hey, Mr. Levine. Smells great."

"Thanks. You and the family joining us for dinner tonight?"

"Not tonight. We can't."

"Of course. Another time." Then, turning to Hannah, "I'm going to need you guys to run dinner over to Mrs. Melvin's for me." Mrs. Melvin had a stroke not that long ago; Hannah's dad cooks for her and some of the other elderly people in the neighborhood. Everyone over the age of seventy tries to get on Hannah's dad's cooking list.

"Dad, maybe you should start charging for your meals. I mean, not a lot, but it could help," Hannah says.

Mr. Levine puts the wooden spoon on the trivet. "I've been helping the folks in this neighborhood for years. I'm not going to start charging money for my meals now."

"But things have changed. E. B. Rule Number 4: Be

flexible. E. B. would say it might be time to reevaluate your business plan." Hannah walks over to the pantry and digs her hand into a box of Thin Mints.

"E. B. is not your parent. Things will work out. Have faith."

I wonder if Hannah's going to tell him everything she heard, but she doesn't. Hannah stuffs a cookie into her mouth and two into her pocket, and we leave the kitchen.

I trail Hannah into the garage. I want to say something comforting and helpful, but all I can think about is the sheet of dust covering the floor.

Hannah either doesn't notice or doesn't care about the dirt everywhere. She sits on the gray concrete and hands me balls of colored rope.

"Cut four orange, four green, four red, and four pink."

I measure the strands against the white rope Hannah gives me and make clean cuts. "Can I get a blue one?" I dig into my pocket and hand her my money.

She shoves it into her ziplock bag and writes the amount down on her sheet of paper. There are eraser marks all over the page. I focus on the pegboard on the sidewall of the garage and count the holes that fill one side. Each board's covered with the same number of holes. Really beautiful.

I watch Hannah braid the bracelets for Sophie, Gretta, Ryan, and Miguel, and then me.

I slide the blue rope onto my wrist and smile.

"Peace be with you," Hannah says.

That's the plan.

We exit the garage, leave behind the conversation of uncomfortable things not said, and head to Hannah's room to fill out the application. I realize I forgot to bring the clothes for the photo shoot. I survey her closet and only see varying shades of brown.

"I promise to bring the clothes next time. At least we can get the questions done now," I say.

The smell of her dad's dinner follows us through the halls.

"Okay. After school I filled out the basic stuff," Hannah says, showing me the screen.

Your Information:

Name: Hannah Anne Levine

Address: 88 Morris Lane, Lantern, MA

Date of birth: August 12, 2001

Age: 12

"Then I got to the first question and got stuck. 'Why do you want to start this business?'"

"Okay, well, why do you want to start Color Me Bracelets?" I slide her desk chair over to the side of her bed.

"To help my dad. To be the next E. B. A little of both, I guess."

I take out a piece of paper and begin to make a list of all the reasons Hannah wants to start the business.

"Well, maybe I should answer the last question first. It asks what I would do with the money. I know that one."

"You're going to have to fill out the whole application anyway, so it makes sense to just do the questions in order." I roll my peace bracelet up and down my wrist.

But Hannah's already typing. She doesn't care about order or lists.

Mid-answer, her fingers stop moving. "Maybe I misunderstood him. Maybe I don't even need to enter this contest. Maybe there's no way we're moving." She gets up from her desk.

"What are you doing?"

"I'm going to ask my dad."

"Now?" I stare at the unfinished application.

She nods.

"Why don't you wait until I leave?"

She grabs my hand. "I'll chicken out if you're not here."

We make our way back to the kitchen.

"Oh good, I'm glad you guys are here. I need you to deliver this to Mrs. Melvin." The counter has a tin tray filled with chicken parm and garlic bread.

I pick up the tray.

"Dad, I, um, heard you talking to Gram the other day. I know you're having a hard time finding a new job," Hannah says in a voice I don't recognize.

I put the tray down.

I hold my breath and wait for Hannah's dad to tell her what my mom didn't tell me. That there's nothing to worry about.

He doesn't.

"I'll find a job. You've tasted my chicken parm. No one can resist," Mr. Levine smiles as he adds garlic and onion to his next batch of sauce.

"What if you don't?"

"I will."

"But what if you don't? Will we have to move?"

I wait again for Hannah's dad to tell her what my mom didn't tell me: *No one is leaving*.

He doesn't.

I pick up the tray and we head out the door.

14

perfect doesn't travel well

HANNAH AND I SLIP into the side yard of Mrs. Melvin's house, and sit cross-legged on the steps to the back door, setting the tray down next to us. The cement feels cold against my legs.

"You okay?" I ask, swallowing my own frustration. I don't get why our parents can't just tell us that no one is leaving and everything's going to be okay.

She shakes her head no.

"We'll figure something out. You can't move," I say. The dead silence lingers in the air. "Kate thinks my mom's never coming back," I finally say.

"What do you think?"

"I think she's wrong."

Hannah reaches for my hand.

I push back the sadness that's creeping up from my toes. "I really miss her."

"Why don't you visit her in Toronto?"

"Yeah, maybe," I say. I know she's right, but perfect doesn't travel well. I keep that part to myself.

We sit like this until we hear Mrs. Melvin's voice through the open screen door. "Hannah! Hannah!" Mr. Levine must have told her we were on our way. We pop up and grab the food.

"Hi, Mrs. Melvin. I'm with Molly. We have your dinner." We step into the kitchen, and I lift the tray of chicken parm onto the mauve countertop as Hannah hands Mrs. Melvin the foil-wrapped garlic bread. The farmer painting winks at me from behind the kitchen sink.

"Oh my, that smells delicious," Mrs. Melvin says. "Why don't you girls stay for a while? We can start a new Scrabble game, the three of us."

She's already sitting at the table turning over the letters and mixing them up. "Heavens, I forgot my glasses and can't see a blessed thing. Would you dears grab them for me? They're resting on my nightstand in my bedroom. It's the second door on the left at the end of the hall."

"Sure." Her glasses are on top of the novel *Carried Away by Love*. On the cover is a picture of a handsome man with a woman in his arms. I pick up the book and show it to Hannah. We both laugh.

The drawer to the nightstand is open.

"Did you find them?" Mrs. Melvin calls from the kitchen.

"Um, still looking," I say, putting down the book.

Hannah slowly pulls open the drawer a little wider. I'm hoping it doesn't creak. Hundreds of fifty-dollar bills and a ballerina statue swim in the bottom of the drawer.

"I thought they were on the stand to the left of the bed. Not the ones on the right—those are for driving. For goodness' sake, I couldn't see a single tile through those lenses."

Hannah nudges me.

The bills are crumpled and scattered. *Does no one understand the concept of a wallet?* I look in again. *Or a bank?*

Hannah whispers, "No way Mrs. Melvin even knows how many bills are in here." Then she leans back to peek into the other room. "She's still sitting at the Scrabble table. I bet she wouldn't even notice if some went missing."

I pick up Mrs. Melvin's glasses.

Hannah grabs my arm. "Wait. The contest entrance fee."

"Don't," I say.

"You know my dad's never been paid for his cooking. Never. Not a dime. And if you think about it, this money wouldn't even cover the cost of the meals we've brought her. In fact, Mrs. Melvin probably owes *us* money."

"Don't, Hannah. It's wrong."

"But I would only use it to help my dad, and then I'd pay it back." She looks at me as I continue to shake my head. "Didn't you ever do anything wrong so you could do something right?" Hannah asks. "Ever?"

That's a trick question.

The doorbell rings. I hear Mrs. Melvin talking to someone.

Hannah peers into the money drawer.

"Don't," I repeat as I walk out of the room.

When I make my way back into the den, I hand Mrs. Melvin her glasses. "They were right where you thought they were."

"That's better," she says, putting on her wire-rims. "Now I can see everything."

There's a tall boy around my age with brown curly

93

hair standing next to a now-beaming Mrs. Melvin. "You remember my grandson, Nate. He's going to be staying here a while."

"Oh, hi." I cough, thankful I did a food inventory of my braces before I left my house. I think the last time I saw Nate we were five.

Hannah walks back into the room, her sweatshirt now zipped. I stare at her, but she avoids my eyes and smiles at Nate.

"Hey." He stuffs his hands in his pockets.

"Where are you from?" I ask, trying not to think about the cranberry juice stain on the right corner of the sofa or how Nate's *Save the Whales Save the World* T-shirt makes his eyes look like spring grass. I barely notice the four pimples decorating his forehead.

"DC."

"His parents are wrapping things up there. They'll move here permanently in a couple of weeks," Mrs. Melvin says.

"Until then, I'm crashing with Gram." He puts his arm around his grandmother.

She smiles. "He's enrolled at Lakeville School. Isn't that where you girls attend?"

As Hannah nods, her uneven bangs flop in her eyes.

Mrs. Melvin pats Nate's shoulder. "He's very smart."

Hannah looks up at the white clock stuck to the checkered wallpaper and says, "I should head home."

"What about Scrabble? Nate can join us," Mrs. Melvin says, already back at the table.

"Next time. I have a science test tomorrow," Hannah says.

I try to decode her words. I didn't think she even had science tomorrow. Did she take the money? Hannah turns away. Then I look out the window and see the Deno's truck driving down the road. "My dinner is about to ring my doorbell. I'm sorry, but I have to go also."

Nate smiles.

A dimple.

15

i see you

I RACE HOME AND meet the Deno's guy at the front door. Shiny crater skin and hair that has no business being in a ponytail.

I put the pizza on the table and go to the sink to wash my hands. I used to just wash my hands, and then I started washing my hands a lot, and now I scrub them raw.

Soap. Water. Scrub. Rinse. Good. *Not yet. Again.*

Soap. Water. Scrub. Rinse. Good. *No. Again.*

Soap. Water. Scrub. Rinse. Good. *No. Again.*

Soap. Water. Scrub. Rinse. Good. *Finally.*

I dry my hands on the towel. "Put Spider back in his cage and make sure you wash up before we eat," I say to Ian. He stands hip-high, his curly blond hair capping at my waist.

"Why do you do that?" he asks, his aqua-blue eyes staring at me.

"I wash my hands before I eat so they're not dirty."

"No. I mean why do you do it over and over again?"

You're little. You're not supposed to notice. Nobody else sees me.

"I guess I just want to get super clean for our yummy pizza. Come on. The sooner you return the creature to his cage and wash those paws of yours, the sooner we get to eat pizza," I say, praying I can reroute the conversation.

"He's not a creature," he says as he runs to his room to put Spider away.

Success.

When he comes back down with clean hands, I help him take a slice of pizza and pour him a glass of orange juice.

"Thanks," he says. He proceeds to pull off and eat all the cheese, orphaning the tomato sauce on the dough, which he refuses to eat. Eating with Ian is like watching a science experiment that's gone terribly wrong.

"Feeling better?" I ask, taking a bite of my slice.

He nods, and he says, "I miss Mommy."

Sometimes I forget how little he is. "Me, too."

"I miss brinner." Our once-a-month breakfast-for-dinner tradition. Pancakes, fried eggs, bacon, and sausage.

I give his hand a gentle squeeze. "It'll be okay." I fold my napkin in half. It doesn't feel right. I hand it to Ian, who doesn't even notice the crooked line.

Quiet fills the space between us as Ian catches the dangling cheese with his fingers. I stare at him wondering what it would be like if Mom was here.

My thoughts are interrupted when Ian wants to know if I will dig for worms with him.

He used to do this with Mom. They called it their annual bug expedition. The thought of putting my hands in the dirt makes my school lunch rise in my throat. I cough. "Not now, Buddy. Maybe another time." I want to be the kind of big sister to him who digs in the dirt, hunts for worms, and slurps the cheese off pizza, but I just can't.

I fold another napkin. *Nope.* And another. *Nope.* And another. *Okay.* I lay the fork neatly on top of my napkin. *A little closer to the plate.* I move the fork. *Better.*

"I see you," the little voice across from me says.

I didn't realize he was watching me.

"I see you, too. We're sitting across from each other. It would be magical if we couldn't see each other."

"No. I saw you fold your napkin a ton and make sure your stuff's all neat and in a row."

Caught.

"I like to be neat. That's all."

He inhales a long strand of mozzarella cheese through the hole in his mouth where his tooth used to be. "It's weird."

I know.

Pause.

"No, weird is eating only the cheese off your pizza."

"That's not weird, it's yummy." Ian smiles, scooping up another strand of melted cheese.

Crisis averted.

"You should try it," he suggests.

"I think I'll stick to eating the whole slice."

Ian's eyes glow and his lips smile like the world is awaiting his next move.

My thoughts of envy come to a crashing halt when his greasy fingers graze my knuckle.

"That's disgusting! Don't put your dripping, dirty hands on me. PLEASE." I know this means another session at the sink washing my hands. I'm so hungry and tired. All I want to do is finish my pizza, do my homework, and go to sleep.

I walk over to the sink.

Soap. Water. Scrub. Rinse.

Again.

I change the subject. "The next time you even think about coming into my room and playing with my glass collection, don't!"

"But they're so pretty. Especially the horse," he says sweetly with a mouth full of cheese. The black horse was from Ian. Well, technically it was from Dad, but Ian picked it out for me. Up until a year ago, I had a poster of a black horse above my dresser. Every Saturday morning, Ian would climb onto my bed and ask me to tell him a story about Harry the Horse. Harry went on many adventures with Ian and me.

When I redecorated my room before middle school, I took down Harry's poster, got an orange shag carpet, and painted my walls vanilla cream and my ceiling green. I wanted my walls fresh and clean. No more posters. A week later, Ian showed up at my bedroom door with a wad of newspaper. He handed me the printed ball and told me it was a birthday present, although it wasn't even close to my birthday. When I unwrapped my gift, I found a black glass horse.

My anger melts. He's so little. Innocent.

"Maybe this year you can take me down to Bridgeway Farms again and I can ride the black horse," Ian says, wiping his cheesy face with the backs of his hands.

"Maybe." I slide my glass to touch the lip of my plate.

Last year, I held Ian's hand while he sat on top of the horse and walked him around the fenced-in area at least a dozen times. When we got home, my shoes were caked with mud and my hands were filthy. I didn't even care.

I miss that.

16

the smallest of peeks

THE NEXT NIGHT WHEN I tuck into my bedroom, my thoughts trail to Mom. When I was little, she read me poems to music, and I'd dance and twirl around the room. Maybe when she calls next, we can Skype like Kate and Kevin. That way she'll see me and remember that she wants to come home. After our last conversation, I sent her a text with a pic of me attached. I was wearing our matching birthday boots. She hasn't texted back yet, but I hope she'll send me a picture of her. Maybe she'll be wearing the *Best Mom* pin that Ian and I gave her when she left. (Kate had refused to sign the card. She said, "Best Moms don't leave their kids for a job.") I spray the I Love You Forever perfume on my clothes and wonder if Mom still smells like jasmine and mint.

I sit at my desk and work on my slam poem. I move the words around, cross them out, erase, and begin again. Round Two is on Friday. There's so much to do. But I can't get it right.

I grab my notebook and write another Me-poem. Unseen and honest.

I'm not the girl I used to be
I don't know what's happening to me

The sting of hurt it burns my eyes
I organize and tell more lies

Share my fear, it's not forbidden
To tell the truth that's deeply hidden

Someone find me, where did I go?
Can you see me? I need to know.

I sit back and wonder if anyone can see the real me anymore. Then I wonder if anyone should.

My homework begs for my attention. I need to create a posterboard story of the Civil War. The scissors aren't in my drawer.

"Kate!" I yell.

No answer.

"Kate!"

Nothing.

I leave my room and find Ian helping Spider-Man save the video-game world. Kate's in the basement; the only sign of occupancy is the R&B music escaping from the crack underneath the closed door.

I stand for a minute and listen to the music.

Knock. Knock.

Nothing.

Again.

Knock. Knock.

"Go away."

"Kate, I need the scissors."

"They're in my room."

I pause, wondering if that's really all I want.

I decide it isn't. She's my big sister. "Can I, um, talk to you about something?"

"Not now. I'm Skyping with Kevin."

"Please." *Don't shut me out. I really need you.*

"Later."

"It's important."

"Later, I promise." The annoyance in her voice is less hidden now.

I'll still be crazy then. I walk away from the closed door and pick up a rare photograph of my family that sits on the table in the hallway. It was taken when we went skiing in Vermont. The snow was falling and we were laughing. I envy the girl in the picture.

I inhale deeply before I enter Kate's room. It's a mess. An empty Cheetos bag on the floor and half-finished water bottles on her desk, dresser, bed, and nightstand. She may look like Mom, but the stuff-littered-all-over gene she got from Dad. I step over the jeans she wore two days ago and grab the scissors that are sitting on top of her jewelry box. The other day she said she got something special from Kevin for her birthday last month, but then went all secretive. I take the smallest of peeks inside the jewelry box. There's a black rope bracelet with a small red star.

As I take a closer look to see if it's inscribed, my heart shatters into a million pieces. I can't believe what is lying next to the bracelet.

17

rainbow of
beautiful colors

THE BEADED NECKLACES KATE and I made for Mom are floating in the bottom of Kate's jewelry box next to the bracelet Kevin gave her. I feel my anger rising from someplace I don't recognize. She had no right. The necklaces were a gift for Mom. They weren't Kate's to take. They don't belong here. I reach in and grab mine, then I grab both. I roll them between my palms four times and leave the room quietly, closing the door behind me. I'm halfway to my room when I realize I left the stupid scissors. Back to Kate's room, get the scissors, close the lid to the jewelry box. Check the lid. No one has to know.

I run into my room to find the perfect hiding spot for the necklaces. A safe place away from Kate. I take out my metal locker—a gift from Papa Lou. It has a lock. I grab the small key that I tucked into my orange socks in my bottom drawer and slide it in. *Click.* The locker opens. Inside is my favorite ruler, a handmade birthday card from Hannah, and the note Mom left for me when she headed north.

Dear Molly,

    I know this is very hard. For all of us. But it's important to me that you know how much you are loved and how much I love being your mom. Remember that I am not running from, but going to something. The year will fly by. Visit often.

    I love you.

Mom

I stare at the note and then at the necklaces. I sink into my bed and remember the day we gave them to her. It was Mother's Day and the house smelled like the roses Dad had bought for Mom. Kate and I were in Kate's room beading the surprise necklaces for Mom. Mine was a pattern: Red. Red. White. White. Black. Black. Until I ran out of red beads. Kate insisted it didn't matter and I could just add more black or white to the back. She said Mom's bushy hair would cover it and no one would even see that part. But I couldn't. I *needed* to continue the pattern.

Kate's necklace was done. It wasn't a pattern and she didn't care.

I love that about her.

I asked if I could have her red beads. Unfortunately, they were in the middle of her necklace.

She looked at me for a long time. Then said, "Sure," and dumped her finished necklace on the bed and handed me all the red beads.

I remember wishing that I didn't care. Wishing my necklace could be a rainbow of beautiful colors.

In any order.

I tuck the necklaces safely into my locker and lock the latch. When my plan works and Mom returns, I'll give these back to her. She won't leave us again once she sees the necklaces.

*

I WALK DOWNSTAIRS AND out the door. I need some air.

Bridgett's standing outside my house. She grabs my hand and leads me to the curb to sit down. "Thank God you're home. I so need to talk to you," she says. The sun has already set, so the trees look lost against the dark sky.

"What are you doing here?" I ask.

"My mom had a meeting at some guy's house nearby, so I asked her to drop me off. I tried calling, but you didn't answer. So I just came by." She stuffs the newspaper in my face. "A true obituary emergency."

"You know there's no such thing, right?"

She nods, like *of course*, but rattles on breathlessly anyway. "Section D, page fourteen, four paragraphs and picture, the obit of a forty-eight-year-old who got shot going to choir practice. Apparently, it was a case of mistaken identity. Same page, half-page write-up about a sheriff and his wife who were gunned down in their home while eating chicken pot pie. Then, same section, page fourteen, column seven, tucked into the last line, is Mr. Gerald Nathanson, a seventy-three-year-old man who died in his bed three days ago."

Bridgett pauses like I'm supposed to understand.

"Gerald barely got a mention and no one even knew he was dead! The others got photos and glowing remarks about their life's accomplishments because they got shot. Do you see?"

Still nothing.

"So now we either have to die young, die famous, or get shot while eating chicken pot pie to get a decent mention in the obits."

I start to laugh. "I would have thought this would make you happy. Before you assumed you could only get a good write-up if you died young or famous. You've just discovered a whole new category."

"But I'm a vegetarian."

18

today is the day

BEEP. BEEP. BEEP. BEEP. My alarm sounds at 6:00 a.m. I quickly slap the button. Silence. My dad still thinks I naturally wake up early. I started setting my alarm about three months ago, when my organizing and cleaning began getting in the way. It feels like it takes me longer and longer to get ready each morning.

Rise and shine.

Kate and I need to take Ian to school this morning. The other day, Dad said something about a big interview that he can't reschedule.

I pull back the covers and pray Kate hasn't noticed the missing necklaces, then I slip my right leg and then left out of bed. Right leg and then left out of the pajamas. Right arm and then left out of the tee and over the head. Fold neatly and place in the hamper. Close the lid. Check the lid. Open the lid. Close the lid. Check the lid.

Now to pick out my outfit. I grab my chocolate-brown corduroy pants and my pink-and-brown long-sleeved tee. Right leg, left leg. Right arm, left arm, head. I straighten my shirt and stand in front of the mirror. Shoot. It's wrinkled. I can't wear this! I pull off the shirt. Right arm, left arm, head. Turn it right-side in, fold it, and place it neatly in my hamper with a note that says, "Please iron." It takes me four tries to get the note just right.

6:10 a.m.

Luckily, my brown-and-cream sweater is clean. I put that on and glance in the mirror. My hair looks like Medusa's. I pick up my brush. Right side. Left side. Back. Again. Right side. Left side. Back.

Again.

No.

You have to!

Right side. Left side. Back. *Again.* Right side. Left side. Back. *Again.*

6:20 a.m.

Socks to match. Right foot. Left foot. Brown boots. There's dirt on the bottom of the left one. I walk quietly to the bathroom, pick up a towel, wet it, and wipe clean the bottom of my left boot. Then the right. Just in case I happen to miss the dirt. Then the left. The right. The left. The right. The left. The right.

Tick. Tock. 6:30 a.m.

I walk back into my bedroom to make my bed. I strip off the fluffy cream comforter and tightly pull the bottom sheet. The silky feel of the wrinkle-free fabric makes my heart hop. I run my palms over it again and again.

I pull the white-and-chocolate-checked top sheet up and let the airy feel of the sheet brush against my cheek. *Pure. Free.* I lay the sheet neatly atop its twin, and again run my fingers across the plane, removing any remaining creases.

6:45 a.m.

I'm making good time. I hear Kate turn on the shower. I know in twenty minutes she'll be downstairs ready to go. Last step. I grab my blanket and spread it over my bed. I pull the top right, bottom right, top left, bottom left. *Smooth.* Almost done.

My door noses open. I turn to look. Before I can react, Oscar jumps on my bed and burrows under my comforter.

"Get off!" I yell at my eighty-pound fur mound of a dog. His tail stops mid-wag and anchors between his legs. His ears slump. He hops off the bed, runs to the corner of my room, and melts into the carpet with a whimper.

"Sorry, big O. I know you didn't mean it."

I look at my bed that now looks like Dad's version of *no big deal.* Hives pepper my neck.

I plunk down on my untidy nest and rest my face in my now-clammy hands.

"What's going on?" Dad pokes his head into my room. "Is everything okay?"

"No, everything's not okay. Look at my bed. Oscar did this." My hands wave over the mess that is now my bed.

"Honey, it's—it's—"

"What? No big deal?" I say, mimicking my father.

"I understand it's upsetting, but it's getting late. I have to leave and all of you need to get to school." He pauses and motions for me to stand. "Let's go. I'll help you make it."

I look at his unshaven face. "Are you sure?"

"Yep. If it has to be done, then let's do it."

Love you, Dad.

He lifts up one end of the comforter to help me straighten it.

With my bed made, Dad closes the door behind him. "I'll see you downstairs." The smell of his pine cologne lingers. I take a deep breath. I have five minutes to brush my teeth.

Not likely.

I walk into the bathroom to brush my teeth. I concentrate as I carefully spread the green-foam toothpaste across my toothbrush. *Get it straight and you won't have to do it again.* Slowly I squirt the paste along the bristles. Nice and perfectly aligned. My stomach grumbles. My hand starts to shake. *No. Concentrate.*

Slosh! The toothpaste falls off my toothbrush and into the sink.

Again.

Four times and I finally get my flawless line.

Exhale.

When I get back to my room, I stand in the middle

and stare at my perfectly aligned glass menagerie, my wrinkle-free bed, my neatly folded clothing, and realize that I can't keep doing this. Things are getting worse. I'm losing control. I have to tell someone.

Today.

19

say cheese

I LOOK DOWN THE stairs and see Dad digging in his brief-case for something. *Maybe I should tell him.*

He looks up. "It's late, people. Everyone downstairs now." He stares at his watch. "I've got to go. It took me six months to get twenty minutes with this guy."

Maybe not Dad.

"Go. We'll be fine," Kate says.

He surveys the two of us. "You sure?"

We nod.

"Okay, then. Love you guys. Text me when you get Ian to school."

I grab three protein bars from the pantry. I toss Kate the sugar-free peanut butter one. She says, "Thanks." I exhale a little. Seems the rescue-of-the-necklaces remains a secret safely hidden in my closet.

I look around. "Where's Ian?" I ask.

She shrugs.

"Ian," I call upstairs.

Nothing.

I run back up to his room. Ian's sitting on the floor in his Spider-Man costume holding his pet hedgehog. "Hey, Buddy, you might want to change. It's time for school."

"I'm not going to school today. Spider really missed me yesterday."

"I know, but he'll be right here waiting for you when you get home. And isn't Raheim in Mrs. Washington's kindergarten class, too?"

He nods.

I wish Mom was here. At twelve, I'm just not good at this parenting thing.

"I have an idea," I say. "Look up, smile, and say cheese. Both of you."

Click.

I take a picture of Ian and Spider, and print out two copies in Dad's office. I tape one to the outside of Spider's cage and hand one to Ian. "Put this in your backpack. It will be like Spider is coming with you to school."

He gives me a toothless grin and stuffs the picture and a photograph of Mom and Dad from his corkboard into his bag, returns Spider to his cage, puts his little hand in mine, and says he's ready to go to school.

When we get downstairs, Kate starts to say something about his Spider-Man costume and I shake my head. Subject dropped.

Mrs. Washington's kindergarten room looks just like I remember it. I hold Ian's hand and I bring him over to the block corner. I take a moment to organize the blocks by color so it's easier for him to find what he's looking for. Red. Yellow. Green. Blue.

I look around the room. Mrs. Washington is talking to Elle's grandmother, and other moms and dads are still hanging around their kids. Not Kate. She's already outside. As I get up to leave, Ian tugs at my pant leg.

"Two more minutes," he pleads.

We build a castle and I'm relieved when Raheim walks over dressed as Batman. Ian doesn't even look up when I leave.

Outside, Kate's sitting by the large maple tree we

used to have snacks under when we were still in elementary school and Mom was still living in the United States. As I walk over, I take a deep breath and decide to tell Kate. She's my sister. She can't disown me. No matter how crazy I am or what I may have stolen from her jewelry box.

"I used to come with Mom to drop you off at kindergarten," Kate says. "You spent the entire time organizing the blocks then, too."

"Actually, about that, I, um . . ."

"Mom should be here. Ian needs her," Kate says.

"I know, but she had to go to Toronto to keep her job." I think back to the morning she left. I prayed for a flat tire on the way to the airport or a canceled flight, but neither happened. Mom had clasped my hand around my turquoise sea glass, hugged me close, and said, "Hold on tight to this until I get back. It's only for a year, Molly. You can visit anytime and we'll talk every night at six. I promise."

Kate stops walking. "She could have gotten a different job. People do it all the time."

I think about Hannah's dad.

"Kevin's mom got laid off and within a month she

found something else. She didn't just leave her kids and move to a different country."

"Mom didn't leave us," I say.

"Yes. She did. And the sooner you get that, the better!" Kate barks.

"You're wrong. She went to a *job*. And when that's over, she's coming home." *Maybe even sooner if everything goes according to plan.*

"You always did believe everything she said. Like when she promised to take us to see *Wicked* in New York City, and then bailed the day we were supposed to go. Or the time she was supposed to leave work early so we could ride the new roller coaster at Six Flags, but then asked for a do-over when she got too busy."

"She had the flu before New York and some big juice guy came into town the amusement park day." Pause. "She's never lied to us, Kate." In my mind I wonder if promising to come home on a particular date and then not coming home on that date is a lie.

"She said the separation from Dad was temporary," Kate argues.

"It is. What's your point?"

"Moving to Canada seems pretty permanent."

"She didn't *move* there for good. It's for one year, at most."

"I'm not even sure I want her to come back," Kate says as she plucks a pinecone from the ground.

"You don't mean that." I search her face for a speck of untruth, but don't find any.

"I might." She throws the pinecone across the lawn of the school and it bounces off the top of the picket fence.

Panic lodges deep in my gut. If Mom thinks Kate doesn't want her back here, she may never come home. "Did you tell Mom that?"

Kate shakes her head no.

I should feel relieved, but I don't. I just feel scared that everything is falling apart. Spinning.

Out.

Of.

Control.

✳

WHEN WE GET HOME, Kevin's waiting in the driveway to take Kate to school.

"Want a ride?" he asks me.

"Nope, I'm good." I go into my own room and close

my door, thankful for Late-Start Thursdays. I pop in my earbuds, take out my ruler, and organize my glass figurines. It's not until I leave my house and see Hannah waiting for me, that I realize she's the one.

She's the one I need to tell.

Everything.

20

my right side

"HI. I LIKE WHAT you're wearing. The glasses are totally working with your outfit," Hannah says as we head to school.

"Thanks." I readjust them so they stop sliding down my nose.

"How did it go with Ian?"

"Other than him refusing to leave Spider, and insisting on wearing his Spider-Man costume, it went fine." I decide to leave out the argument with Kate.

"Spider-Man. Hmm. A bold choice."

I look her in the eyes and squeeze her hand. The eye-squeeze combination is our signal that something's important. When my mom first told me about her juice job in Canada, I gave Hannah the combo.

This is it. I'm going to tell her. Everything. She's my best friend. It'll be okay.

But before I can bring the words to my lips, Mrs. Melvin walks over to us. "Good morning, girls."

She's wearing her creamsicle-colored slippers.

"Morning," Hannah says.

I give my best fake smile that keeps in all my lies.

"Hannah, dear, with Nate arriving last night, I forgot to give this to you." She holds out some money. "Your father told me about your business and I think that's quite ambitious for a young lady. I would love to buy a bracelet that's red and green and yellow."

"Oh, thank you, Mrs. Melvin." Hannah takes the rolled money and stuffs it into the ziplock bag.

Still no wallet, but at least she's moved away from the bug jar.

I decide that I'm going to tell Hannah and start with the glass figurines. Or maybe I should begin with the hand-washing at the lemonade stand or the pizza dinner with Ian. No, my glass collection.

When Mrs. Melvin walks away, I say, "Hannah, there's something I have to tell you."

She gives me the go-ahead nod, but then tears roll down her cheeks.

"What's wrong?"

She wipes her face. "Nothing. I'm fine. I swore I wouldn't do this. You go," she says.

But I can't. It's a sign. I should wait.

"No, seriously, what's the matter?" I ask.

Her dad got another rejection from a local restaurant, and then this morning she got an e-mail from Mr. Samson, her drama teacher, about a new book she needs to buy for class and a message from the tennis coach to order the team jacket for twenty-eight dollars. "I can't ask my dad for the money. And if I use what I make from my bracelet business, I'll never get enough money for the contest entrance fee."

I feel sad all over for her. "Here." I pull my wallet out of my bag and hand Hannah the babysitting money I made last summer. I was saving it for this cool five-drawer storage box with built-in dividers that organizes your papers and stuff, but I'd rather give it to her.

"Are you sure? I mean, I don't know if I can pay you back." She starts to twirl her hair. "I mean, if I win, I can, but if I don't . . . I, um, don't know."

I take her hand and wrap it in mine. "We're cool. It's yours."

She hugs me tight. "You are the Best. Friend. Ever."

She gives me a full-braces smile. Eyes, too. "Thanks, Mol, I mean it." She adds the money to her baggie.

Hannah's tears come to a slow roll. "Now, your turn. What's up?" she asks.

As we cross the street, the school comes into view, and Hannah navigates around a muddy puddle and ends up standing on my left side.

I wish she hadn't done that.

I wish she knew.

That.

   Nothing.

     Works.

       On.

         The.

           Left.

21

frozen

I CAN'T MOVE. I'M frozen like an ice sculpture. My confession is far from my lips.

Why'd she do that? My left side. It feels wrong, so uncomfortable.

What do I do now?

Hurry, think of something.

Hannah's forehead's all wrinkled. She's talking, but I'm not listening.

Our eyes lock like it's a staring contest, but it isn't.

My body feels like I'm wearing my right shoe on my left foot. I don't know what to do.

Slowly, Hannah moves back.

Again, I'm standing on her right side. She really is my best friend.

"Of course I can hear you. I'm fine." I swat her flailing hands away from my face. I look around, hoping no one noticed. I pause to gather the pieces of my lie. "I must've gotten a rock in my boot and when I stepped down it pinched the bottom of my foot."

Hannah looks at my boots, which are firmly planted on the cement sidewalk that's clear of dirt. "Yeah, that can hurt. Do you want to sit and shake it out?"

Thank you.

I know it's another sign. First Dad, then Kate, now Hannah. Every time I try to share what's hidden, something goes wrong. Maybe I'm not supposed to tell my secret.

To anyone.

I sit on the bench outside of school, slip off my boot, and shake it out as if it truly held the very thing digging into my soul.

I stare at Hannah. Her uneven hair blowing in the wind. I tighten my hair clip.

She tilts her head.

"Molly, what were you saying before, you know, we, um, sat down?" Hannah asks.

22

another weird thing

BEFORE I GET A chance to say anything, Bridgett walks over. "Molly, Mac's having a party Saturday night and I'm in charge of the invites. Want to come?" She snaps the pink bubblegum that's popping around in her mouth.

Hannah coughs. I know it's fake.

Bridgett completely ignores Hannah.

"Well"—I look at Bridgett, then at Hannah, back to Bridgett—"only if Hannah can come, too."

Bridgett says, "Really?"

"Really," I say.

"Whatever," she says, never once looking at Hannah.

I know Bridgett can be kind of prickly. Sometimes. To some people. But for me, for now, she's easy to hang with. She doesn't see me the way Hannah does. She doesn't see through my weird habits. All she cares about is dead people, obituaries, and herself.

The bell sounds. Bridgett and the herd of kids stampede past us.

I slip my boot back on and we head into the school.

"Thanks," Hannah says.

"You'd do the same thing for me."

We walk down the hallway side by side. "What did you want to tell me?"

"I don't even remember," I say. Lost my nerve. Too many signs screaming, *Don't Tell! She'll think I'm crazy and weird and never want to hang out with me. No one will want to be with me. I'll be the girl everyone avoids. I'll be that girl.* In fifth grade it was Liza Lempkin. She was fine and then she was absent. For a really long time. There were whispers about her being hospitalized. Not like cancer-sick, but the other kind. Super sad and sleepy all the time. She didn't return to school for the rest of the year. When she finally came back last year at the start of sixth grade, I saw her sitting alone at lunch. I should have sat next to her.

Besides, even if I wanted to tell Hannah, which I've

decided I don't, how could I even explain what's happening to me?

"Enough about me." I turn to Hannah to change the subject far away from me and my confession. "We need to talk about last night at Mrs. Melvin's."

"Not now," she says, pointing to Bridgett, who's standing at my locker. "I promise we'll talk later. Maybe you can come by and practice your poem and help me with my pic and the rest of the application. I'm almost done with questions one and three."

"Sounds good. And about Saturday night at Mac's, let's go together. It'll be fun," I say. While we walk toward class, a new weird habit finds me. I start counting my steps by multiples of two. *2, 4.* Thankfully, my brain defaults to even numbers, but I don't want another weird thing. *Leave me alone.* But it doesn't listen. *6, 8, 10, 12.* It's another sign. Now I *know* I can't tell Hannah. Or anyone. Ever.

"I don't know. I mean, I'm glad you got me invited, sort of, but I'm not sure I want to go. Those girls don't even like me."

"They just need to get to know you," I say. I hung out at Bridgett's two weekends ago. Bridgett and Arianna went on about how Hannah and I are nothing alike. They told me that I could be in their trio, but not Hannah. I told them Hannah's been my best friend since Eagle Nest Day Camp, and they didn't mention the trio thing again.

"Anyway, I told my dad I'd help him deliver meals Saturday night."

14, 16, 18, 20, 22, 24. Stop counting.

Between numbers I manage to say, "I'm sure your dad can handle the deliveries without you. It'll be fun. And if you hate it, I promise we'll leave."

Count. 26, 28, 30, 32, 34, 36.

"Come on," I say. "I think Jared's invited."

Hannah's had a crush on him since fifth grade. I struggle to smile and count.

38, 40.

"Maybe. I'll talk to my dad later."

42, 44, 46, 48, 50. We're at our classroom.

Hannah walks in. I can't. Not yet. I'm at 50. It's even. That's good, but it's not a multiple of four. And, if I stop now, that's five numbers. Five is a terrible number. I hate myself. This doesn't even make sense. Stay focused. Even numbers. Multiples of four.

I keep walking.

Then Hannah yells out, "Molly, where are you going?"

My joy disappears like water down a drain.

I feel my face turn brick red. *I know what I'm doing.*
I didn't miss the class. I walked by it on purpose. Next
time I'll count by fours. Fours are better. They're made
up of two twos. The square is sixteen and the square
root is two.

"Where did you go?" she asks, running toward me.
She stares at me a second longer than necessary.

I look away. I wish I could tell Hannah. Everything.
But I can't.

"Nowhere. I'm fine." Fake smile, fake laugh. Start
again. *4, 8, 12, 16.*

"We have to talk." She pulls out her ziplock bag, and
floating at the bottom is a fifty-dollar bill.

23

stop it! stop it!
stop it! stop it!

"OKAY, CLASS." MS. P. writes something on the whiteboard. "Put your notebooks and papers inside your desk. We're having a short pop quiz."

Groans ripple through the class.

Ryan calls out, "Ms. P., we really haven't gone over the material enough to fully prepare us for this quiz."

20, 24, 28, 32. I say nothing. I'm sitting, but the numbers still flood my brain. They won't stop. It's a struggle to keep up Fake Molly while I count.

"Hands down. The quiz is just a review. No more talking. Clear your desks and take out a pencil."

I open my pencil box and carefully remove a newly sharpened No. 2. I run my fingers along the flawlessly smooth tip. Joy hugs me like a new, stark-white bedsheet just out of its packaging.

Ms. P. passes out the paper, still warm from the printer. "You may begin."

36, 40, 44, 48. I like pre-algebra, so I'm not nervous until I look down at my paper. There are eleven word problems on the sheet. *Eleven.* Eleven is a terrible number. It's odd. It's prime. In fact, it could be *the* worst number. I lose count again. I close my eyes for a moment. *Think good, even thoughts. Begin again. 4, 8.* I open my eyes, ready to start. But I can't. It's not working. My good, even thoughts aren't erasing my worried, Tilt-A-Whirl feelings. *12, 16, 20, 24.* I look at my watch. 9:09 a.m. *Okay. I'll wait until 9:14 a.m. to start. That'll be a lucky time. It contains the number 4 and if you add together the digits 9, 1, and 4, you get 14! Perfect.*

I hear the scratchy sound of my classmates' pencils on their papers. *28, 32.*

9:14 a.m.

Start.

1) There are twenty-four crayons to be shared among four students. One quarter of the crayons are primary colors.

How many primary-colored crayons can each student have?

Is Ms. P. doing this on purpose? Does she hate me? The answer is obviously one and a half crayons. But who breaks their crayons? Who has one and a half of a pomegranate red or spring-grass green or middle-of-the-ocean blue? 36, 40, 44, 48.

I begin to write my objection to the question. *Oops. Made a mistake.* I flip my pencil over and erase what I've written. A big black smudge replaces my mistake. I bite the inside of my cheek. I erase again. The black mark becomes a larger, charcoal-gray cloud at the top of my paper. I open my pencil box and gingerly pluck another pencil. I turn it over, admire its shade of never-used pink eraser, and rub it over the rain-cloud smudge on my paper. I rub and rub and rub and rub. *52, 56, 60, 64.* It's getting lighter. Lighter still. Almost. Rub. *Oh, no!* It ripped. The paper tore right through my dusty puff. *Why's the room so hot?* A drop of sweat slides off my forehead and lands on my desk. *Not now. Come on. Get it together.*

Wipe the sweat.

Fix the paper.

Count. 68, 72, 76, 80.

Take the quiz.

Be normal.

I reach back into my pencil case and remove a roll of tape. I'll just patch the tear and begin again. I pull a piece of tape and rip it straight along the sharp edge. *84, 88. Crooked.* Let me try again. *No. Again. Again. Again.*

"Molly, is everything all right? You seem distracted." Ms. P. leans over my desk.

"I'm fine. You just startled me."

"I apologize for that, but I was referring to your quiz. Is everything okay?"

"Uh, yeah. It's just my eraser was broken and then my other eraser made a hole and now I have to fix it." *92, 96.*

Shut up! I silently scream at the person who sounds like me, but isn't me at all.

"Well, move along. There are only five minutes left. This quiz is meant as review. It shouldn't take too long, and relax, you're not being graded on the condition of your paper."

Fake smile, push up my glasses that are now halfway down my nose.

I look around the room just long enough to notice Hannah's eyes on me.

Stop it! Stop it! Stop it! Stop it!

As the five minutes wind down, I neatly write my name on my quiz and turn in a blank, taped-up sheet of paper to my teacher.

100.

24

hangers-on

"WE NEED TO TALK. In private," Hannah whispers to me after Mr. Benny, the cafeteria man, dumps a scoop of mashed potatoes on my tray.

"I know. As soon as we find a table." I scour the lunchroom, willing the numbers to stay put inside me. "Not this one. It's so dirty. How about that one over there?" I point to the table to the far right.

"Whatever. It looks just like all the other ones. I don't really care. It's the cafeteria. We can either sit at this ketchup-splattered table over here or that pizza-greased table over there. I just need to talk to you," Hannah says.

"But we don't have to sit at the most disgusting table." Fingers crossed—a clean table means no counting.

"It's just a place to eat our high-in-mystery-meat, low-in-nutrition school lunch." Hannah follows me.

"No, not that one, it's gross, too."

"Molly, there's nothing wrong with this table. It's no dirtier than it's ever been," Hannah says, pointing to the table next to us.

"Other than the hard peanut butter chunks stuck to it," I say on my way to another table.

"Well, soon we'll be eating lunch standing up."

"Here, this one's perfect." I wipe off the table with my napkin. "Don't you girls agree?" I ask Bridgett and Arianna, who are already sitting at the table. They nod in unison.

"If you were going to wipe off the table anyway, why did it matter where we sat?" Hannah asks over the rumble of her stomach.

We slide into our seats, and like ants to a picnic, Ryan and Greg walk by.

"Hey, Molly," Ryan says, waving and slowing down.

"Hi," I say with my best beauty-queen smile.

"I like your sweater, and, uh, your mashed potatoes look good," Ryan says. Big metal grin on a beet-red face.

"Thanks."

"Well, um, have a good lunch."

"Yeah. You, too," I say.

When they walk away, our table bursts into fits of laughter.

"You've got some good-lookin' potatoes," Hannah says to me.

Our laughter explodes all over again.

Someone taps me on the shoulder. It's Nate.

"Hey, can I sit here?" he asks, nodding to the spot next to me.

"Hi. Sure." I make room for him to sit down.

The girls' eyes fix on me. Then him. Then me again.

"This is Nate. Mrs. Melvin's grandson."

"Hi. You new?" someone asks.

Nate's dimple is showing.

"Just started this morning," he says.

A chorus of giggles.

"How's your morning going?" I ask.

"Well, so far okay. It took me a while to find Room 107. But the burgers are good."

"If you need help finding your other classes, let me know." Hannah grins. So hard I notice she has a piece of lettuce wedged between her braces. I give her a look and discreetly point to my teeth. She picks up the signal and wriggles the lettuce free. She mouths, "Thanks." Then asks me, "Why did Ms. P. come over to you during the quiz?" The numbers have been quiet, but the sound of Ms. P.'s name brings them back to life. *104, 108, 112, 116.*

"Who's she?" Nate asks.

"Our math teacher," I say. "She thought I had a question."

Lie.

I look down at my plate and notice my lumpy mashed potatoes oozing into my green beans and my burger. *120, 124. Why today? I'm so hungry. I don't want to be weird around Nate. It feels like I'm trapped on the top of a Ferris wheel with no way down.*

"What did you think of it?" Hannah asks as she sinks her teeth into her big, juicy burger.

"Of what?" I ask. I notice the potatoes dangling off the bottom of Hannah's hamburger bun.

"The pop quiz?"

"It was fine." I wish I could be like her. Maybe if I take the burger out of the bun I can eat it. *128, 132.*

Through bites, Hannah says, "I thought it was pretty easy, but I got stuck on problem six. What did you get for that one?"

"I don't remember."

Lie.

I remove my burger from the bun, examine both sides for any hangers-on, and happily cut off a piece.

"Why aren't you eating your bun?" Hannah's eyebrows raise at the sight of a naked burger.

"Not that hungry." *136, 140.*

Another lie.

"Really? I'm starving. Anyway, problem six was the one where you had to figure out how many starfish washed up on shore. I got seven, but I'm not sure if that's right. Is that what you got?" Hannah licks the mashed potatoes off the bottom of her bun.

"I really don't remember."

Nate's plate is clean. Burger, bun, gravy, mashed potatoes. All gone. He turns to the girls at the end of the table. "It was good meeting you guys." Then, "Molly and Hannah, I'll catch you later."

"You know how to get to your next class?" Hannah asks.

"I passed it on my way to the cafeteria, but I have to stop at the office first to fill out some forms. Thanks." He picks up his tray and trails out of the lunchroom.

Hannah turns back to me. "Why won't you tell me how you solved problem six? What's the big secret?"

"I told you, I just don't remember how I solved the

equation." I can't tell Hannah that I turned in a blank quiz. *144, 148, 152, 156.*

I look around the lunchroom. Jimmy "The Beef" Durkins, Reggie Lyons, and a few other football players are sitting at the table next to ours. Eating. Laughing. Normal.

I want to be normal.

Bridgett's shrill voice jars my attention back to our lunch table.

"You have to give Arianna her money back for the bracelet," she barks at Hannah.

"There are no refunds," Hannah says, taking a bite of her ketchup-soaked fries.

"Look, she got a pink one. The love thing didn't work out. You're a liar and your business is a joke."

"I'm sorry she didn't find love. But if you read the rules, you would know that you can't—"

"I don't care about your stupid rules. Just give her the money back," Bridgett shouts. Other kids start to stare.

I need to say something, do something, but I can't. *160, 164.* I'm consumed with how I'm going to eat my lunch now that the burger, potatoes, and beans have melded together. Then Bridgett turns to me. "I told you she's like the woman on page fifteen of the obits who died alone after cheating all her friends and family out of their money."

All I can finally say is, "Bridgett, don't." *168, 172.*

Then she asks, "You got the blue one. But tell me, Molly, have you found your peace?"

25

say something

I NEED TO SAY "yes" or "shut up" or *anything*. Instead, the color drains from my face. I yell at myself to lie. *176, 180, 184, 188*. But I realize this is the one thing I can't lie about.

"See, it's a fake. You're a loser." Bridgett says, getting up and walking away.

Hannah's not the fake. I am, I say to no one.

∗

AFTER SCHOOL, I'M WAITING at my locker for Hannah when Ms. P. calls me into the classroom.

"Molly, I need to speak with you about your quiz today. What happened?"

The numbers creep in. *4, 8, 16, 20*.

"I don't know," I say softly. The thought of Hannah

overhearing our conversation knocks my volume down a decibel.

"Molly, it's not like you to turn in an incomplete quiz. Is everything okay?"

24, 28, 32, 36.

"Yes. I told you when you came over during the quiz. My eraser broke and made all sorts of black marks on my quiz, so I had to use another one from my pencil box to wipe away the mess from the paper. I rubbed and rubbed and just when the paper was coming clean, it ripped. So, of course I couldn't turn in a ripped quiz. Luckily, I had tape. I tore off a piece and fixed the sheet. Then I put my name at the top, and unfortunately, that was when you said it was time to put our pencils down."

40, 44.

"You completed none of the problems."

"You really didn't give us adequate time." *48, 52.*

"Molly, everyone else finished, and you're one of my top students. I just want to make sure there's nothing wrong."

"I had an off day."

Not totally false. I'm having an off life.

"That can happen. I'll give you a chance to retake the quiz. I want to make sure you understand the material."

"Thank you, Ms. Piper."

56, 60, 64, 68.

My head throbs as I walk to my locker. Hannah's standing there. "Sorry I'm late. I had to help Ms. P. with something," I say.

Another lie wriggles out.

"Oh," Hannah says.

I search her voice to see if she believes me. She has her angry eyebrows on.

"First, I can't believe you didn't stand up for me with Bridgett," she huffs.

At least she believes that I was helping Ms. P.

"Second, we need to talk about the fifty dollars. My working theory is that Mrs. Melvin meant to give me a five and handed me a fifty by mistake. She had all those fifties swimming around her drawer, but she can't see without her glasses, and she wasn't wearing them when she gave me the money." Her angry eyebrows slowly fade.

"The fifty was from this morning?"

"Yes. Oh wait, you thought I took that money from her drawer?"

I shrug. It's hard to accuse her of anything while I'm counting and hiding every real thing about myself.

"I didn't. I was tempted, but I didn't steal the money. Mrs. Melvin gave it to me this morning. But what if she didn't mean to?"

"Just ask her."

"If she gave me the money but didn't mean to, and I use it, is that still stealing?"

72, 76, 80, 84.

"Why don't you just ask her?" I repeat.

"Because she might take it back, and then I won't be able to pay the entrance fee, and then there will be no chance that I can help my dad."

How can she just say exactly what she's thinking?

I hide my envy. *88, 92, 96, 100.*

"About Bridgett, I'm really sorry about what she said. I love my bracelet."

"You should have told her to shut up. I can't believe you said nothing."

Now she seems mad with a dash of sad. I knew I should've done something, but the mashed potatoes ruined everything. "I was spacing about the slam. I'm sorry. Don't be mad." *188, 192. Wait, what was my number? Can I just start here? Are there rules to the counting?*

"Then do something about Bridgett. She's *your*

friend." Pause. "And just so you know, I'm not giving one penny back."

196, 200. I nod, close my locker, and we head home. I try to change the subject. "The party will be fun."

She stops walking and stares at me. "Are you kidding? I'm not going to the party now. Ms. Death will be there."

"You can ignore her and just hang with me." *204, 208.*

"You should have thought about that before you sat there and said nothing," she says.

"I told Jared you were going and he seemed psyched he'd see you there."

Hannah says nothing. But she's twisting her mouth, which I know means her no is now at least a solid maybe.

26

goodnight moon

WHEN I GET HOME from school, Dad is multitasking
with the phone and the computer. He gives me a slight
nod and a how-was-your-day-but-don't-answer-me-now
wave. Ian's back to not feeling well and is flopped on the
couch, and Kate's at work.

I feel Ian's forehead with my hand the way Mom used
to do. He's lukewarm and his eyes are shiny, and not in
the good way. "Hey, Buddy, how are you doing?"

He grunts, rolls over, and falls back to sleep.

Ian starts to snore. I kiss his forehead, drop my bag,
and go for a walk. I pass by Mrs. Melvin working in her
garden. She's bent over the tomato plants with a big-
brimmed hat resting on her head. "Hello there, Molly,"
she calls.

"Hi." I wave and look around.

She comes over with a basket. "Here, want some? Freshly picked." Her hand shakes a bit as she holds out the sun-warmed cherry tomatoes.

"Thanks."

"Your new glasses really suit you. Come sit with me a minute. I need a rest." She heads over to the wooden rockers on the back porch as if I've already agreed.

"Uh, okay."

We settle in and rock with the tomatoes between us. For a moment, I forget everything bad. I realize the counting has stopped. Maybe it won't come back. Ever. I don't question it. Maybe the rocker or the tomatoes or Mrs. Melvin made the numbers disappear. I'm just grateful for the quiet in my brain.

"You and Hannah helped me plant this garden when you were little."

I can't imagine sitting on the cold, wet ground and digging. The thought of the brown dirt stuck to my hands and the dirt wedged under my nails makes the sweet tomato taste bitter. I return the other tomato to the basket.

"It's mum season. I'll need some help getting those potted in the front." She points to a ledge of about twenty mums. Yellow. Burnt orange. And cranberry. "I've already recruited Nate. You girls are welcome to pitch in."

"Sure." I know it's a lie, but I can't tell her the truth.

The front door swings open.

"Hey." It's Nate.

"I was just telling Molly about the mums." Mrs. Melvin gets up. "I need to get out of the sun for a bit. Why don't you take my chair?" Nate lets his grandmother kiss his cheek and then joins me.

Brown curly hair. Dimple. Green eyes. We sit for a while talking about the Red Sox's run for the World Series and the school's lack of soda machines. I fill him in on the good and bad teachers and the kids to avoid. Then I tell him about Mac's party Saturday night.

"Will you and Hannah be there?"

"Yep." I hope that's not another lie.

We rock for a few minutes in silence. I realize we've run out of stuff to talk about. Awkwardness finds its place between us. I say a quick goodbye and stand up to continue my walk to nowhere. When I get back home, Dad's still on the phone, but I have a plan.

I call Bridgett. After she goes on and on about the two paragraphs devoted to Blake McGinty, a country singer who died from a drug overdose, I tell her I won't write her obituary unless she promises to be nicer to Hannah.

"Fine, but technically you're going back on your word. You had already agreed to write my obit if I died first, and now you're agreeing to write it only if I die first *and* I'm nicer to Hannah."

"I'll be sure to include that in your obit."

I hang up and my phone sings its B. B. King reminder— twenty-nine days until what was supposed to be Mom's visit. I write, erase, and write again the lines to my new slam poem. I tell myself to focus. *I need to win. Mom wouldn't miss the banquet. She'll come home.*

To us.

To me.

We'll be back together. All of us.

Then she'll stay.

She wouldn't leave twice.

I get stuck mid-poem. It's not working. The restlessness creeps back in. I wonder if Ian is okay. I rub my fingers across the sea glass and wish my life was different. I wish *I* was different.

The music I downloaded last night fills my room. I'm hoping it calms me. It doesn't. The counting starts again. *4, 8, 12, 16.* The numbers help, but not enough. I look around my room. I know to Hannah, Kate, Ian, and Dad, things look neat, but they're wrong. I dump my sock drawer, re-ball my socks, and organize them by color. White, cream, yellow, orange, red. I stand back and admire my masterpiece. *20, 24. That's a little better.*

I move on to my shirts, pants, shoes, and finally glass figurines. I organize everything and anything. I hear the clock ticking. Time passes. *Is Ian all right now? He's fine. Dad said he just had a cold. But what if it's something worse? Lyme disease, EEE virus, or the bubonic plague. All those illnesses start like a normal cold.* I run downstairs to check on him. He's still lying in front of the television sleeping. I get real close to make sure he's breathing. He stirs, and when he opens his eyes, my face is two inches from his. *28, 32.*

He looks at me funny. "What are you doing?" Ian asks.

"Um, just making sure you don't need anything." *Like medicine, a doctor, or a hospital.*

"I'm kind of hungry."

This wasn't part of my plan. I need to work on my slam poem and make sure my colored pencils are sharpened and in order. From the couch, I see the door to Dad's office is closed. It's article deadline day. I don't bother knocking.

"Want brinner?" I ask.

He pops up and smiles. "I knew it. Is she hiding in the kitchen? My room?"

"Who?" I look around.

"Mom."

"Buddy, Mom's in Toronto. Remember?"

He sinks back into the couch. "I thought she came home to surprise me."

"Why?"

"I thought she came back to make brinner for me because she knows it makes me feel better."

My heart shatters. Like the day she left and he cried so hard into my favorite aqua tee that it left water stains.

"*I'm* going to make you brinner! Pancakes, fried eggs, bacon, and sausage."

He hugs me tight for a long time.

After brinner, I tuck him into bed, and read him *Goodnight Moon*. I'm grateful there are no more boogies on his wall.

"I love you, Molly," he whispers as I leave.

"Love you, too, Buddy."

When I return to my room, my slam poem stares at me, unfinished. Good night counting, good night organizing, good night all weird stuff. I wait, but it doesn't work. I scribble the poem that fights with the numbers for my attention.

In the dark of night I often pray
For normal me to find her way

To see the world
Bent and torn

To love the chaos
And the worn.

In a whisper I count by four
And mourn the me that is no more.

I wait, but the numbers return. *36, 40.* I dump my sock drawer on the carpet and begin arranging again. I have to. I know it's not over. Is this what crazy feels like?

Ms. P. always says, "Knowledge is power." I open SearchMaster and type: *Am I crazy?* No, delete. Be specific. *Like things perfect clean neat.* I hit Enter and hold my breath.

27

in the closet

I RELOCATE TO MOM'S closet. I want her with me when I find out if I'm crazy. The smell of jasmine and mint surrounds me as I settle onto the floor of the closet. I put my sea glass down next to me.

Before I can even look at the search results, the door flies open. Kate stands there glaring at me.

She knows.

"You had no right sneaking around my room!" she growls, her face the color of Mom's disgusting beet juice.

"I didn't sneak around your room. You told me to go in there to get the stupid scissors," I say, hoping she'll go away. *4, 8, 12, 16.*

Unfortunately, she doesn't.

"What did you do with them?"

The numbers scatter and spill. I have to start over. *4, 8.*

She ignores me. "Let me guess, you sent them back to her? Well, guess what? She doesn't want them."

"You're a liar." *12, 16.*

I see the anger seeping out of her, but I don't stop. "You stole them. You wanted to hurt her. You've been punishing her ever since she said she was leaving. Admit it!" I yell. *20, 24.*

Her phone rings and she glances at it, then at me.

"You have no idea what you're talking about. You drag that stupid sea glass everywhere like it's going to magically fix things. You think Mom's working and loves us and in a year everything will go back to normal. Well, guess what, Mol, there is no normal!" She turns away from me and answers her phone. "Kevin, hold on." She covers the phone with her hand and says to me, "Be careful what you wish for, Sis."

She storms away as I yell, "I'm not giving the necklaces back!" *28, 32.*

I inhale Mom's mint/jasmine combo to quiet the chaos that's pulsing through my body. Kate's wrong.

I shove her accusations and lies into a deep, dark well in the corner of my brain, and then open my computer. *36,*

40. I discover 2,310,000 results have popped up from my search. "Do 'Neat Freaks' Have OCD?" "11 Things Messy People Will Never Understand About Neat Freaks." "International OCD Foundation—5 Things OCD Is Not." "14 Beautiful and Perfect Gifts for the Neat Freak in Your Life." "Obsessive-Compulsive Disorder— Kids Health."

My brain swirls. The numbers tumble and then go quiet. Neat Freak. Obsessive-Compulsive Disorder. I remember when I went over to Bridgett's house one time and she laughed at me when I wiped off the table four times. "You're so OCD. That's what your obit is going to say." I laughed, too, but there was a tiny speck inside me that thought, *maybe.*

I need to know. Now. My finger shakes when I click on the article that tells me what OCD is not. Apparently, OCD is not a joke. Good to know, but not particularly helpful.

I move to the top of the OCD Foundation page, to where it says "OCD in Kids," and click. The page opens with a message in big letters across the top: "There is Hope." *Not likely.* Then it asks, "So what is it, really?" *If I knew the answer to that question, I wouldn't be on this stupid website.* "OCD is made up of two parts—obsessions and compulsions." I read on. Some of the stuff sounds like me, but not all of it. I mean, I worry about bad stuff happening to Ian, I like even numbers and want to get good grades, but I don't worry that I will hurt someone by accident or have bad religious thoughts. I read on and on. Then I make a list to see how many of the obsessions I have.

I count up my answers.

Yes: 4

No: 6

Fewer yeses. That has to mean something. *Right?* I read on. It says if I have these thoughts, I likely also do the compulsive stuff. I look at that list. Sure, I do some of those things, but not all of them. I mean, who doesn't wash their hands? And how am I supposed to know how much is too much? And is there some site talking about kids who don't wash their hands enough, because I'd like to share that with Ian?

My brain feels jumbled and full. I think about my family. Ian, Kate, Dad, Nana Rose, Papa Lou, and me. All their weird stuff seems to be about who didn't put the chips back in the cupboard. Mom's neat, but not list-worthy weird about it. Dad's a slob whose only obsession is work. Kate's between a slob and regular and so is Ian. Nana Rose was always saving stuff, but that was just her, and the only thing Papa Lou cared about was Nana Rose.

I read and search and read. One in every two hundred kids has OCD. At least, if I had OCD, I wouldn't be alone. For now, though, my confusion lands on the only decision it can understand. I made a list and have fewer yeses. I should be relieved, but I'm not. Because now I don't know what I am. Maybe just crazy and by myself. No site for that. I stay here for a while longer. Then I search online for articles or blogs or any space where kids are sharing their secrets.

> **PARKER RAY:** I've been counting ever since I learned my numbers. It's time to let go. Even of my favorite number eleven.

Who would love that number? I read on.

> **MARIA F:** Sometimes, well actually lots of times, I'm scared I might hurt or even kill my little brother with my dirty, germ-infested hands.

I sit on my hands.

LYLE G: I lick my palms and slap the wall seven times before I can move into the next room. Yesterday, I got stuck in my bedroom for an hour.

What's with the love of odd numbers?

ANNA: I ate my homework. Literally. I can't stop eating paper.

MICHAEL: I wish that was my problem. I screamed things at my neighbor that I'm too embarrassed to write. And she's a nice person. I just couldn't not.

My phone buzzes. I look at my watch and think it's Mom, but it's Hannah. I hit Ignore. I jump on Facebook and Twitter. The pages open under the name Lynx Lomain. Lynx was the brainchild of one rainy day last summer. Since Hannah's dad and my parents collectively decided to ruin our social lives by banning all social media, we both created fake accounts so we could stay in touch with Benji and Nick from camp. Mine was under the name Lynx Lomain and hers was Miley Martin. Now Lynx is doing reconnaissance. So glad I have her. Some groups are closed, but eventually I find kids talking.

Getting better but can't stop organizing my desk.
Why do people think I can just stop?
Does anyone out there pick at their skin?
I can't eat food that touches other food.
This girl from my school always says she's so OCD
and she's not. I hate her.

Is my list wrong? Are there kids like me? Do they hide like me? Confusion floats to the front of my brain. Again.

I close my computer, leave Mom's closet, and go back to my room. I sit on my bed for a while and let my head sink into my hands. I don't know what to do. Finally, I take out my ruler and make sure the cow, piglet, owl, mouse, and eagle are all evenly spaced.

Exhausted, I fall asleep. Sleep is the only time my worry's quiet. But tonight's different. Tonight it gets into my dream.

Someone's broken into my room. He's lurking in the closet and I feel him staring. I want to scream, but I'm frozen. My eyes scan the room. My glass figurines are scattered; my poems are torn out of my journal and shredded into confetti all over my floor. I hear him counting by threes and laughing. I hear Ian crying in the next room, but I can't move.

I jolt awake. I must've screamed in my sleep because Dad's standing stiff and tall at my door. My clock flashes 2:00 a.m.

"What's the matter? Are you okay?" Dad rushes over to me and feels my forehead, his look of anxiety pouring down on me.

"I'm fine."

Everything is fine.

There's that word again.

"Fine? It's the middle of the night and you're screaming and trembling. Molly, look at your hands!"

My hands are shaking like the Spider-Man bobblehead doll that sits on Ian's nightstand. I shove them under my butt.

"I'm okay. It was just a stupid bad dream," I say, convincing myself. I pause. "Dad?"

"Yeah?"

"For school, we have to find a thing—you know, a disorder that's hereditary. And I, um, found this one called OCD, Obsessive-Compulsive Disorder. And . . ."

What are you doing? You already made a list. Counted. You don't have it. Stop. Talking.

But there's that small speck of me that WON'T SHUT UP.

"Mol, as long as you're not sick, can we talk about your schoolwork another time? It's two in the morning, and I have a big day tomorrow."

"Sure. I mean, I just wanted to know if you knew anything about it. Like, did anyone you know have it? It's, um, hereditary, so a kid wouldn't have it unless someone in her family had it. Most likely."

His sigh is loud, followed by a long empty pause of nothing.

I hold my breath, not even sure what I want him to say.

28

lonely,
the number eleven

DAD SAYS HE DOESN'T know anyone with OCD. "I'm a borderline slob." He winks. "Mom's neater, but nothing unusual." He pauses. "No one comes to mind, but you can ask Mom tomorrow. Maybe she knows more." His face twists at the mention of her. He turns and walks out of my room. In the hall I hear, "I love you."

Now what? Part of me celebrates that I don't have the thing that makes kids lick stuff, but then my happy dance ends. Because if it's not OCD, then what's wrong with me? Is this just some weird version of me?

I grab my journal and write what's crashing in my head.

Not like you.
Lonely raft.

Not like you.
Single tear.

Not like you.
Empty cart.

Not like you.
Burned forest.

Not like you.
Vacant eyes.

Not like you.

Then I hide under my covers and let the salty tears flow into my pillow. *Help me. Somebody. Please.*

*

TODAY IS ROUND TWO.

I inhale all the air I can and wish hard for a different

me. A me who can slam and talk and live without hiding.

But I already know wishes don't come true.

So I check my desk.

Need.

   Everything.

     In.

       Place.

Lucky sea glass.

Sharpened pencils.

New eraser.

Ready.

My cowboy boots scuff the wooden floor, but this time it's harder to tuck the real me away. She won't be ignored. *4, 8.* Last night when I couldn't fall back to sleep, I learned how to weave the numbers in my head into the rhythm of my poem. They're still hidden. No one will even know.

The applause comes to a slow stop as I tap the microphone. I twirl my lucky sea glass in my pocket. I see Hannah and Bridgett in the front row. Not together.

I don't wait for my mind to quiet because I know it won't. *12, 16.* I pray I can keep it together for the next ninety seconds. I take a deep breath in and the words stream out.

Lonely, the number eleven—
frightened, scared, and out of place
Odd

Lonely, the crumpled page—
damaged and without a home
Broken

Lonely, the blue glass whale—
out of line and can't get back
Lost

Lonely, the last song beat—
over when the music's gone
Quiet

Lonely, the lying girl—
hidden behind the glass door
Seen

Lonely, sometimes
just so lonely
Me

I exhale. I did it, I got to the end. And kids are applauding. And snapping. And hooting. I find my seat and listen to my heart and the numbers rapid-fire in my head as the finalists from Mr. Henshaw's class share their poems. *64, 68, 72, 76.*

When they finish, Ms. P. takes the microphone. "The winners of Round Two will be announced on Tuesday morning. The final competition will immediately follow the announcement. Again, great job, everyone."

Bridgett comes over as the crowd thins. "You're definitely going on to the final round," she says. "Just think, Slam Poet Extraordinaire can be added to your obituary."

"Not exactly what I was going for, but thanks."

I look around for Hannah, but she's gone.

"I thought it was kind of depressing, but in a good way," Arianna chimes in.

Then Nate walks up. "Cool poem." Dimple.

I smile. And count. *80, 84, 88, 92.*

"Thanks."

"You heading home?" Nate asks.

I look around once more for Hannah, but still don't see her. Then I remember she said something about an orthodontist appointment right after school.

I nod.

On the walk home, Nate tells me about his friends Jed and Nate B. from DC. Everyone always mixed up Nate and Nate. He smiles and laughs.

I pretend to laugh with him and realize that I kind of have another Molly. Except they're both me.

Then I keep counting. *96, 100.*

He stares at me for a long second. I pray I have something green in my teeth because otherwise he's just wondering what's wrong with this girl. I wriggle my tongue across my teeth. *Nothing.* I do it again. And again. And again.

Please don't see me.

He moves on to a story about Jed and Nate B. and him in some soccer tournament. I half listen and fake smile and count.

I'm grateful when I realize we're in front of Mrs. Melvin's house. She's waiting on the porch for Nate.

"Well, see you at Mac's tomorrow night?" he asks.

I wave goodbye.

104, 108.

29

doesn't look
like nothing

I TURN OFF MY alarm and the sun streams in through the pinholes in my window shade. I hide under my covers. It's Saturday and I hear Dad calling me from downstairs, but I pretend to be asleep. Pretending is something I do well. Too well.

Under my covers, I think about what Kate said. She's wrong. Mom didn't leave us. Kate's just mad. She doesn't get that Mom went to a job. I get it. Most of the time. And when I don't, when I'm scared Mom will forget us, I snap a picture. Like yesterday I took a pic of me and Ian and Spider and sent it to her. She hasn't replied. Yet. But it was late. And I know she's really busy.

My mind switches to Round Two of the slam poetry competition. I pray I make it to the finals. Last night

I slept and slept and slept. Hiding is tiring. I jump online and reread Parker Ray and Maria F. and Lyle G.
and Michael and Anna's stories again. And again. I know
them. Not the real them, but the kids who do all that
weird stuff. I unwrap the plastic from my new journal and
start writing:

In the darkness
There is fear

In the fear
Hope is lost

Beyond the hope
There is me

Imperfect and frightened
Me.

I lie like this for a while and read my poem over and
over again. The sadness wraps me. I don't know what's
wrong with me. I dig in my brain for answers, but find
none.

"What are you doing?"

I peek out from under the covers and see Ian and Spider staring back at me. He's so little, so sweet, and so normal.

"Nothing."

"Well, it doesn't look like nothing. It looks like something." Pause. "Can I do it, too?"

"There's nothing to do."

"Well, you've been in here forever. Daddy says maybe you're sick." He hops on one foot thirteen times.

My stomach flips, wishing for one more hop.

"Are you?" he asks.

I think about how to answer that. Finally, "No." At least, not sick in *that* way. "You?"

He shrugs. "Don't think so. My brain doesn't feel all hot and mushy anymore."

Relief sweeps in.

"Does *your* brain feel hot and mushy?" he wants to know.

I shake my head no.

"Then why are you still in bed? I've already had breakfast and lunch and gone to the car wash with Daddy."

"I was tired."

And scared. And sad. And crazy.

"Oh."

I love that he believes me. He walks over to my glass figurine collection and looks back at me. "Can I hold the zebra?"

I slide out from my covers and wait for the numbers to flood my brain.

They don't. Quiet wins the battle for now. Maybe it's Ian. Maybe he's my shield.

"Put Spider away and I'll give you Beethoven."

When he speeds back into my room, I go over to my collection and gently hand him the zebra. I got the zebra the day Mr. Klein, my fourth-grade teacher, took our class on a field trip to the Parkway Zoo. There was a contest to name the new baby zebra. My vote was Beethoven since his stripes reminded me of the keys on a piano. Hannah and I walked around with Lily, Kyle, Kendra, and Kendra's mom, who spent most of the time on her cell phone. My dad said he wanted to come, but he had a last-minute deadline to meet. The zoo named the baby zebra Wayne, but I bought the zebra glass figurine from the gift shop and called him Beethoven.

"Want to go to the zoo?" my little brother asks, as if that's an actual possibility. As if the thought of dirty pastures and muddy paths and smelly pens doesn't burrow under my skin like a bloodsucking parasite.

"Can't." *Or won't.* "Another day, okay?"

He hands me the zebra back and hugs my middle. I wonder if he'll still love me when he finds out I'm crazy.

I text Hannah that I will come over to work on her application and photo before the party. By the time I get there, I'm late. It takes me four tries to get my sock drawer just the right amount of neat.

"Where have you been?" Hannah asks.

"Getting the stuff for your photo shoot."

Half true.

Hannah stands in front of me in beige sweatpants and a mucus-colored long-sleeved tee that says *I Love My Camper.*

"You can't wear that for your contest photo," I tell Hannah as I take inventory of her closet. Beige pilled sweater. Brown turtleneck. Tan corduroys. I open the large suitcase I brought full of clothes. "Take off the sweatpants from fifth grade and the shirt from your gram and put these on." I pull out a dark gray suede vest I borrowed from Kate when she was at work (I figured she's already mad), jeggings, and a great pair of boots. Hannah hugs me. Super close. She stares at me too long.

Is my crazy showing?

I tighten my hair clip and pull up my socks. "What are you doing?" I ask.

"Nothing." She looks away and wriggles into the clothes I brought for her.

"You look cute," I say.

"Thanks, you too. I like your hair in that silver clip. And, um, your poem yesterday was really good."

"Thanks." I smile, but not with my eyes. It's fake. Like me.

Hannah twirls her hair and says, "I liked it a lot. It was just kind of sad."

"I guess." I'm not looking at her.

"Is everything all right?" she asks.

"Everything's fine." I refold the other two shirts in the suitcase.

The lie hangs.

I ignore it and grab my phone. "Do you want me to take those pictures?"

Hannah nods.

I snap a few photos of her outside her house holding the Color Me Bracelets sign I made for her with my stencil kit. The wind's blowing, and her bangs fly in the breeze. We move inside to her dad's office. Hannah tapes the poster to the wall behind her dad's black vinyl chair, and then sits at his desk looking very businesslike while I take a few more pictures.

Her smile drops on the last click. She's looking down at the desk.

"Doesn't E. B. have some rule against frowning?"

She holds up a letter addressed to her dad. It's another job rejection.

"I don't want to move."

I think about Canada and Mom and how perfect doesn't travel well.

"I know," is all I can think to say. Then I show her my favorite photo of her from today. The first one of her sitting in the leather chair at the big wooden desk. Her braces are hidden, her hair is tame, and the sign is straight.

I close the office door when we leave. Hannah attaches the pic to the application file and answers the rest of the questions. She dumps her ziplock baggie on the bed and we realize she still doesn't have enough money for the contest entrance fee.

"I gave you all the money I have from babysitting," I say, counting the number of boxes on her wallpaper even though I know there are one hundred forty-six.

"What if I use Mrs. Melvin's fifty for the contest fee

and write her an IOU?" Hannah doesn't wait for me to say something. "It's not like I'd be stealing or anything. I mean, she gave me the money."

"She gave you *some* of the money for sure, but maybe not *all* of the money."

"But maybe she did."

"Maybe. So just ask her," I say like a take-charge kind of girl who knows how to fix a problem. A girl nothing like the real me.

30

the kiss

WHEN HANNAH AND I get to Mac's house, his mom's standing at the door of the basement with an unlit cigarette dangling from her lips. "Trying to quit," she says as we pass.

I hold my breath and pray the basement is clean.

As I step down the stairs, the numbers find me again. *4, 8, 12, 16.* It's hard to count and act and smile and talk.

Nate's already here. Bridgett pulls me to the side of the room as soon as I'm downstairs and whispers, "That Nate kid is totally cute. Will you introduce me?"

20, 24.

"He was at our lunch table the other day," I say.

"*Everyone* was at our lunch table."

"Okay, I get it."

I walk over to Nate. He does look good. Green tee. Green eyes. Dimple. "Nate, this is Bridgett, Bridgett—Nate."

When I turn around, I see Jared over by the chips and Hannah on the other side of the room. I happily stand alone with my numbers—*28, 32, 36, 40*—until I hear, "Grape or cream soda?"

I grab the cream soda from Hannah and notice the wallpaper on the far right corner of the wall is peeling. *44, 48, 52, 56.*

"Jared's here," I tell her, pointing over by the chips. "You should go talk to him."

She shrugs. Hannah and I go through two sodas each before Greg comes over. He wants to know if we think the Red Sox will win the World Series this year.

"Of course," I say.

"No way," Ryan says. He grew up in New York. Last year, he did his Person in History report on Derek Jeter.

We debate the pitching and batting rotation. Greg and I are in agreement that this is the year the Sox will win it all.

"What do you think?" I ask Hannah. She's a huge Sox fan, but has said nothing for most of the conversation.

"Um, yeah. Sox will win it all." Fake smile.

I give her a what's-going-on? look, but she ignores it.

Ryan grabs the bowl of chips, and we all move to the couch. It's clean and empty. Until Tim Conway and "The Beef" plunk down next to me. The floral couch fits four kids or two linemen comfortably. But not four kids *and* two linemen. *60, 64, 68, 72.*

When I get up, I can see Nate and Bridgett talking outside through the screen door. One of my favorite songs comes on. I'm about to see if Hannah wants to dance when Mac comes over and just stands next to me. Says nothing. The numbers dash in my brain. *76, 80, 84, 88, 92, 96. Count and smile. Count and smile.* I scratch hard at a cut on my ankle. *100, 104.* Kind of wish he'd say something. Anything.

"I've got to go ask Hannah something," I finally say.

Half true. I can tell Hannah wants to leave; she keeps twirling her hair and twisting her ring around her finger.

Before I can get to her, Bridgett comes back inside. And she's smiling. I barely recognize her. B doesn't really do happy.

"You may need to write my obituary," she says, smile still firmly planted on her face.

"I don't want to state the obvious, but you seem to be breathing." *108, 112.*

"I might die from kissing him," she says.

"You kissed Nate?"

"More than once."

Hannah interrupts. "We need to talk."

"Right now?" I ask. *116, 120.*

She nods. I leave Grinning Bridgett and follow Hannah into the bathroom. Coconut air freshener with a rust-stained rim. Streaked-mirrored medicine cabinet. Lip of the linoleum flooring peeling. I gag back the overwhelming need to puke and decide to toss out the idea of a mouthwash search. The numbers tumble and I have to begin again. *4, 8.*

"We need to talk *in here*?" I ask. "Can't we do this somewhere else? Anywhere else?"

"No." Hannah locks the door behind us. She closes the lid of the toilet and sits down. I stand. No sense trying to figure out what's clean in here. *12, 16.*

My phone sings the blues—twenty-seven days until Mom's original-now-maybe return.

"What's that?" Hannah asks.

"Nothing," I say as I tuck my phone back into my

pocket. "What do you need to talk about that we have to do it right now in the bathroom?" I ask.

"I can't believe you."

I look around. "What did I do?" *20, 24.*

"You introduced Nate and Bridgett."

"Well, actually they sort of met at school. I just re-introduced them. What's the big deal?"

Hannah looks annoyed. Then I realize the problem. She likes Nate.

"Wait a minute. I thought you liked Jared." *28, 32, 36, 40.*

"I did, but not anymore," Hannah confesses as she picks up the who-knows-how-many-people-have-used-it brush.

I swallow my desire to grab the brush and flush it down the toilet. "You should've told me about Nate."

"Does she like him?" Hannah asks.

I see B's grin seared in my mind. "Don't know for sure." Not exactly true, but I don't want to hurt Hannah. I tighten my hair clip. "Look, I'm sorry. I didn't know you liked him. I'll talk to Bridgett." I wait for her to seem relieved or at least less annoyed, but she doesn't. "Can we leave the bathroom now?" I ask. It's getting harder to count and talk. *44, 48, 52, 56.*

"No."

"Look, I didn't know," I repeat.

"It's not that. Well, not *just* that." She looks at me like she's trying to unravel the Caesar cipher encryption. "What's going on with you?"

31

the postings of
lynx lomain

THERE'S A LOUD KNOCK on the door. Ryan needs the bathroom. Something about three grape sodas in need of an
exit plan.

Hannah stares at me, waiting for my answer, but
gives up when Ryan's knocking turns into a continuous
banging.

After that, we leave the bathroom and the party. The
car ride's quiet; Hannah's mad is wedged between us.
When I get home, I dial Mom. No answer. I dial three
more times, just to be sure I dialed right. Still no answer.
I wish she was here. Maybe she would know what's wrong
with me. The numbers find me. *4, 8.* I spray Mom's
perfume and open the door of her closet. Kate's already
sitting on the floor. Crying. Surrounded by crumpled

tissues. The last time I saw Kate's sadness leak out was when she was in fourth grade and broke her leg skiing. We stare at each other like a game of chicken.

"What do you want?" she asks, blowing her nose.

"Nothing." *12, 16. I want to be normal.*

Technically, we're still fighting about the necklaces, but I can't leave her like this. I sit down next to her and she moves in closer to me. The mad slips behind the leaky sadness.

"What's wrong?" I can't imagine what could bring her to a twenty-tissue count. *20, 24.*

"Kevin broke up with me." Her mascara trails down her cheeks. She grabs another tissue and thankfully drags the pile of dirty ones to her other side.

"I'm really sorry." I don't know what else to say. I've never had a real boyfriend. Matt in fifth grade doesn't count. It lasted two weeks and I ended it when he came in smelling like old cheese. "He's an idiot." *28, 32.*

A smile escapes under a newly drenched tissue. "Thanks."

She braids my hair and I tell her the long list of stuff that annoys me about Kevin. *36, 40.*

We sit like that for a while, then she says, "I'm sorry I yelled about the necklaces."

"I'm sorry I yelled, too, and called you all sorts of terrible names."

"You did?"

Then I smile and she laughs.

"But I don't get why you took them from Mom." I need to understand this. None of it makes sense to me. "We made them together. For her."

"We did. But, Mol, I didn't take them from her. She left them here."

The air drains out of my lungs.

Kate holds my hand. "I found them in the back of the closet the first time I came in here after she left. They were on the floor. I didn't want you to find them. I knew her leaving them would make you sad. So I took them and put them away in my room."

After a while, Kevin's signature ringtone blasts in the closet. Immediately, I know I'm going to regret telling Kate all those things about Kevin. I leave Kate in the closet and go to my room.

How could Mom have left the necklaces behind? Everything feels upside down. Nothing makes sense. I log on to Facebook as Lynx. I take off my blue bracelet and lay it on my nightstand. *Be brave. Write something.*

LYNX: New here. Can't stop counting. Or organizing. Or worrying that my little brother is going to die. It's getting harder to hide. Help.

I hold my breath. Not sure what I even want to happen.

PARKER RAY: Hi newbie. Yeah I do that. Count by 11s.

LYNX: Hate disorder. Hate dirt. Hate odd numbers. Hate that all that matters. So tired of hating.

Maria F. joins in.

MARIA F: Hey there. I hate germs. And germs. And germs. And that I hate germs.

This goes on with Parker Ray and Maria F. and me until Dad walks in. I slam my computer shut. Facebook is strictly off-limits. Another tip he got from those parenting magazines.

"What?" I ask.

"It's late. I'm heading to sleep. You need to do the same."

I nod. As if that can happen before I straighten my figurines, my socks, my everything.

When the door closes, I text and call Hannah, but she

ignores both. I know she's mad about the Bridgett-Nate thing and my unconvincing rendition of *everything is fine*. But it's not my fault. I didn't even know she liked Nate. As for the other thing, Fake Molly obviously needs to sharpen her acting skills.

I check on Ian in his room. He's breathing and sleeping, despite Spider scurrying around his cage, building a huge shavings pile in the right corner. I leave and finally fall into a fitful night's sleep.

When I wake on Sunday, my dreams slip fast from my thoughts. I check my phone. Still nothing from Hannah. I know she's upset about Nate. So I grab a protein bar and walk over to Hannah's to apologize again. In person. When I get there, her dad's in the kitchen baking an apple crisp. The kitchen smells like my own kitchen used to a long time ago.

"Hannah's working on the business in the garage."

"Thanks, Mr. Levine. Smells great." He tells me it'll be ready in thirty minutes, so I should stick around.

I open the door to the garage. Hannah's sitting on the floor, her back to me. She doesn't move.

"Hi." I walk in, the real me tucked safely away under layers of lies. My stomach flips.

Hannah says nothing.

The smell of week-old trash smacks me in the face. Still don't understand why Hannah set her business up in the garage.

"Look, I didn't know you liked Nate." I slowly move around to see her face. I want to know if she has her angry eyebrows on. "Your dad said you were—"

I stop talking. My eyes widen.

Hannah's sitting on the cement floor with Lynx Lomain's Facebook page open.

All. My. Posts. Totally. Visible.

My breath catches somewhere deep in my throat and hives dance all over my neck.

The numbers pour out. *4, 8, 12, 16.*

She looks up at me. A tear rolls off her chin and lands on her lap.

My world tumbles. Fast. I feel like the last victim in *Masked Horror Night* when she realizes it was actually her best friend who's killed everyone. "What. Are. You. Doing?" It comes out low and garbled and through gritted teeth. The anger bursting from the place Gerry the Yogi tells us to find our Zen. My worry ticks. *20, 24, 28, 32. Is Ian really okay? Maybe I should call Dad.*

"I'm sorry," she says. "I knew there was something wrong no matter how many times you told me everything was fine. I remembered Lynx and thought maybe you'd post something as her. You know, like what's going on with you."

I stare at her. No one knew I was Lynx except Hannah. No one knew my password. Not even Hannah. But she knows me. Too well.

I can't believe she's still talking. "It took me a few tries to get the password: lemonadeonlaurellane. But it was so easy, I figured you actually *wanted* me to know. I thought this was your way of telling me."

She's smiling. So proud of herself. She stands up and reaches for my hands. "Please talk to me."

My whole body is in shock. I yank my hands away from hers and scream *DON'T* with my eyes. I text Dad—

> Ian ok?

—hit Send, and stuff my hands into my pockets. *36, 40.*

She moves closer to me.

I step back.

> *Keep.*
>> *Your.*
>>> *Distance.*

"Who's Parker Ray? What's the matter with Ian? And

what are you counting? I mean, I'm with you all the time and don't know what you're talking about. What's going on?"

My thoughts jumble. I say nothing. *44, 48, 52, 56.*

She continues in a soft voice, "I just want to help."

My anger grips my entire body. "This is how you help me? You hack into my account? Sneak around my life? Read my private stuff?"

I stare at my phone. No reply from Dad.

"Only because I was, I mean, am, um, worried about you. Please talk to me."

"Talk to you! Not now. Not ever. You are *not* my friend. Friends don't do what you did." *60, 64, 68, 72.* I focus on the pegboard and count the holes.

My phone buzzes. It's from Dad. Ian's spiked a fever.

32

longest stretch of mad

I HAVEN'T SPOKEN TO Hannah in twenty-eight hours. This is our longest stretch of mad. There's no school today because of a teacher workshop, so I'm at Bridgett's. Hiding. With her my stuff is well hidden. She doesn't see me. The real me. I can't face Hannah. She sees me and I'm not ready to be seen.

My phone buzzes. New message.

> Please don't stay mad. I really am sorry. You're my best friend. I only read that stuff because I care about you. I'll be making bracelets all afternoon if you want to come over. Call me.

I don't.

"So what did Hannah want when she yanked you away from me at Mac's?" This is the third time Bridgett has asked.

"Nothing important." Same answer.

Bridgett raises her right eyebrow. "You sure? Maybe *she* wanted to kiss Nate."

She's fishing for information. But I won't do that to Hannah. Even if I'm mad at her.

"You always say how great she is and that she'd do anything for you, but I don't see it."

I continue to flat iron my already straight hair.

"You've kind of been acting weird today. I mean, if you flat iron that one piece of hair again it's going to fall out." The numbers begin to tumble into my head.

She's not supposed to notice me. That's why I'm here. "I'm fine." Fake smile.

"Okay." Everything goes back into hiding.

There's the Bridgett I know. Totally unseeing.

She tells me again everything that happened with Nate at Mac's party. Then she says, "Mrs. Zelda Zane, died at the age of seventy-five, leaving a husband of fifty years, three children, five grandchildren, and two great-grandchildren. Zelda and her husband, Greer, worked together in the film production company they started forty years ago. They were known for their films about tormented souls."

She keeps reading, but I stop listening. I think about the movie Zelda and Greer could make about my life. How would it end?

"The Holocaust, the Great Depression, and world hunger were the backdrops for a number of their films." Bridgett looks up from the article. "You see, we need to be someone to have people remember us when we die."

"Why?" I'm tired, and tired of hearing about dead people. Not sure I want anyone to remember the real me. I glance over at the pumpkin muffin crumbs on the counter. "Why do you care so much about dead people and their obituaries?" I've asked this question before and have never really gotten an answer.

But today's different. Bridgett folds the newspaper obit of Mrs. Zelda Zane so that it's face-up. "My dad."

Huh? She's never talked about him. "What about him?"

"He died," she whispers.

"I'm so sorry. I didn't know." I knew her dad left them,

and I knew she and her mom moved here from New Jersey, but I didn't know anything else.

"It was a long time ago. He left my mom and me and moved to Florida about five years ago. I was sort of okay with it. I mean, they fought all the time anyway, so I figured at least the fighting would stop and I'd get to go to Disney for all of my school vacations."

She takes a bite of her muffin and continues. "I asked him if I could come visit that winter break and he said his place wasn't ready, but that I could come in the spring. A month later, he died in a weird boating accident."

I stand up and wipe the crumbs off the counter. Four times. She pauses for a minute and stares at me.

The numbers creep into my head, now fully awake. *4, 8, 12, 16.*

"A few years ago, I was looking for something in my mom's dresser and found a box of his stuff, including his obituary. Since my parents weren't together, and his parents had died, and he was an only child, some random person wrote the obit. 'Michael Kent died at age forty-three in an unfortunate boating accident off the Florida Keys on Friday, January 16th.' One line. No mention of me. No mention of his life. Nothing. Just that he had died."

"That's terrible. I'm sorry."

"It was like he never lived. Never mattered."

20, 24, 28, 32. In that moment, I realize Bridgett is hiding, too.

33

walking around
in the dark

WHEN I GET HOME from B's, I grab my glasses, sit down, and write my own obituary.

> Molly Rose Nathans died at age twelve and is survived by her loving parents, sister Kate and brother Ian, his pet hedgehog, and their dog. Her mother immediately flew in from Toronto to join the family. Molly also leaves behind her best friends, Hannah and Bridgett. Molly was a wonderful slam poet and neat child until a rare illness took her life. It attacked her brain cells, making her

think she was going crazy. She
dreamed of being a doctor someday.

It takes me a long time to get it right. The rare illness seems to fit. I'm not sure OCD is technically correct and I haven't found anything else in my search that makes sense. In this draft, I add Bridgett because she'll definitely be reading my obit and I don't want her to feel left out. I also put in Spider to make Ian happy. Hannah was my last add. I'm still blood-boiling angry, but I couldn't leave her out. My craziness senses something is happening. I fold my obituary neatly four times and tuck it into the right corner of my drawer next to my ruler. I try to work on my poem in case I make it to the final round, but my mind's crowded with numbers instead of words.

B. B. King blasts my daily reminder on my phone—twenty-six days until Mom's fingers-crossed-still-planned first visit.

Oscar nudges open the door and stands in the middle of my room staring at me. Then he barks. I realize I forgot to feed him. "Come on, boy." Oscar and I go outside to get his food from the bin on the porch. Bridgett's standing there.

"You have to stop doing this," I say.

"Doing what?"

"Just showing up."

"Well, I tried calling, but you didn't answer."

I look down at my phone and see four missed calls from B. "Oh, sorry." I realize I was writing my obituary when she called.

"It's cool. Do you notice anything different about me?" B asks.

"We just saw each other. What could possibly be different?"

"Just look. Real close."

I stare at her hair, her face, her cranberry zip sweater, her woven belt, her bleached jeans, and her black leather tie boots. "You parted your hair on the opposite side."

"Anything else?"

Isn't that enough? That's huge. "You have a small run in the bottom right corner of your sweater and your left pointer finger is missing most of its nail polish."

"Okay, all of that is weird and wrong. No, check out my earrings." She slides her long chestnut hair out of the way.

"How was I supposed to see those hiding in your hair?"

"My dad gave them to me before he moved. I thought I'd lost them. I mean, I searched and searched and searched my entire house. Mom was pissed. I tore through her jewelry box, nightstand, and special Dad box—which I never even knew she had. Apparently, she saved her wedding band, a letter he wrote to her when they were engaged, and a necklace he bought her when she turned thirty-five."

I count how many times B spins the lizard earring in her right lobe. "So where did you find them?"

"This is the weird part. I swear it was like his spirit or something."

"Whose spirit?"

"My dad's. After our talk at my house, I went to check my phone, and sitting next to it were my earrings." She crosses her arms and waits for my reaction.

The numbers crowd my brain, making it hard to find space for actual thinking. "Hmm. Wow," is all I say.

"I really think these are a sign from my dad." She can't stop touching her ears.

I would love a sign from *anyone* that everything will be okay.

My phone buzzes. It's a message from Mom.

> Sorry I missed you before. Tied up all day. Need to talk about my visit. Looks like I'm going to have to work that weekend. Will call tomorrow to reschedule. Love you.

My world crashes.

Loud and hard.

That's not the kind of sign I was looking for.

*

AT NIGHT, I CAN'T sleep. I grab a new, lined, crisp pad of paper and begin to write down the numbers spilling in my head.

When I roll over I see that it's 3:00 a.m., and there are eight texts and three calls from Hannah.

> So sorry. Just trying to help. Please please please talk to me.

I close my phone and the counting begins again in my head. *4, 8, 12, 16.*

My stuff's getting worse. Hannah knows I'm crazy. I feel my worry waiting, just waiting for me to forget to count, organize, or straighten. Waiting for me to mess up and then something terrible will happen to Ian. Dad says Ian's fine—just an ear infection—but I don't believe him. Bridgett has shown me obituaries where little kids die from freak accidents, malaria, rare bacterial infections, and other awful things. It could happen to Ian. *20, 24.*

My mind goes to Mom. I wish she was here to watch over Ian. I wish she hadn't just canceled her first visit. I wish she'd never left. Sometimes the house is quiet like an abandoned building in the middle of the night. It seems like Dad, Kate, Ian, and I are all just walking around in the dark. Maybe we'll find each other, maybe we won't. I scratch the scab on my leg and try to re- member what number I was on. *Was it 20 or 24? I think it was 24. 28, 32.*

I grab my glasses, slide my computer onto my lap, and open Facebook. I decide to change my password to hueytheglassracoon4. Hannah's shut off from my ac- count and me. Lynx is mine. Just mine. I scroll down and read a post by Sophia: *Can't stop thinking I'm going to die.* I want to post a comment, but after Hannah's spying, I'm not sure I'm ready for the world to know my secret. *36, 40.* I shut my computer, roll over, pull the covers up tight over my head, and squeeze my eyes shut. Don't want to think about OCD. Don't want to think about Ian. Don't want to think about Hannah. She's mad about Nate and Bridgett, but I don't care because I'm a hundred times angrier at her. She broke her promise. *44, 48.* I flip my pillow over to the side with no tears. I haven't spoken to her since I stormed out of her garage. She says I'm her best friend. She cares about me. She wants to help. I stuff my face in my pillow. It's not fair. She knows. I didn't want her to find out like this. Not sure I wanted her to find out at all. I can't pretend with her anymore. *52, 56.*

I'm losing control of it. I get out of bed and take off my socks, placing them gently into my hamper. I peek into Ian's room. He's sleeping. I move closer. He's breathing. I let out a sigh of relief and slip back into my own bed. *I'm stronger, smarter, better than this. 60, 64.*

Don't.

Give.

Up.

34

hiding in plain sight

WHEN I WAKE UP the next morning, I realize I'm already late. I slept through my alarm and won't get to do half of my stuff. Dad tries to feed me bacon and eggs, Ian tries to talk to me, and Kate thankfully just leaves me alone. She and Kevin are back together. Kevin said he was sorry for being an idiot. At least I agree with him there. I don't want to talk. To anyone. I'm so tired. Last night was an unrelenting march of irrational fears that Ian was going to die in his sleep. EEE. West Nile. Some unknown and unnamed virus. Part of me knew he was just sleeping, but the other part checked on him eight times throughout the night. Quietly, I count under my breath so the constant worry that I need to check on

Ian goes away. *4, 8, 12, 16.* This has to stop. *20, 24, 28, 32.*

I pass Mrs. Melvin's house as I head to school. Without Hannah. *36, 40.* I run my hands through my hair and feel a knot. *44, 48.* Round Two results of the slam competition are being announced this morning. I already hate this day.

Hannah finds me at my locker, hiding in plain sight. *52, 56.*

"Hi," she says. "I waited for you this morning."

I'm silent. On the outside. *60, 64.*

Awkwardness splashes all over her face. "Did you get my messages?"

I stare at her and say nothing. *68, 72.*

"I said I was sorry."

Nothing. *76, 80.*

"You all right?"

I walk away from her.

Josh and Ryan intercept me. I slam my locker before the smell of beef jerky gets on my stuff.

"You're looking at the next slam finalist," Josh says.

"The results haven't even been announced yet," Hannah says.

Don't defend me.

"But we all know who's moving on." Josh high-fives Ryan and jumps up to touch the top of the cafeteria doors. I ignore them and head to class. *84, 88, 92, 96.*

Hannah shuffles next to me. "You seem, um, not like yourself."

I say nothing.

"I just mean that you look tired. I'm worried about you." Hannah reaches for my hand and softly says, "You can talk to me."

My icy stare stabs back and I pull my hand away. "There's nothing to talk to you about. I thought I made that clear the other day. Unless you want to discuss how we're going to explain to Ms. P. why we're late for class."

"Look, I know something's wrong even if you don't want to tell me. You can't stay mad at me forever." She waits for me to agree, but I don't. She tries something else. "At least *you're* not on the verge of moving across the country."

I look through her as worry blankets my brain. *100, 104, 108, 112.* I check my phone to see if there's a text from Dad. "116, 120," sneak out in a soft whisper.

"What? I can't hear you," Hannah says.

Uh-oh.

"I didn't say anything." Now I have to start all over again. I'll never finish by the time we get to class. *4, 8, 12, 16. Sorry, Hannah. Please forgive me. Ian needs me to count.*

"20, 24, 28, 32."

"What? I still can't hear you." Hannah's words slice through me like a razor. I can't start over. I need to look after Ian. I glare at her.

"Go away," I say. *36, 40, 44, 48.*

Please.

She doesn't hear that part.

She looks like a trapped baby deer.

I can't care. I think hard and find my place. *52, 56.*

Don't worry, Ian. I won't let anything bad happen to you. 60, 64. The bell sounds and I find my seat.

Ms. P. holds up two fingers. I try to pay attention. Round Two announcement.

Stop counting.

Now.

"Directly following the announcement, we'll move to the auditorium for the finals."

I check my colored pencils to make sure they're aligned.

"The person moving on from grade seven to compete in the school-wide final round of the Lakeville Poetry Slam Contest is Molly Nathans."

Claps follow. Almost everyone cheers. Hannah runs over. "This is amazing. You're so going to win this."

68, 72. I look away. *She went behind my back. She's not forgiven. She doesn't get to celebrate with me.*

I hug Bridgett, which is weird because she's not a hugger. *76, 80.*

Two fingers up. Everyone quiets and finds their seats.

I look over at Josh. He shrinks in his seat. I feel bad for him. I shouldn't, but I do.

"The crowd was moved by Molly's authentic and emotional recitation of her poem." Warm smile toward me.

I dig deep for my fakest self and smile. I tug on the knot in my hair.

Lily whispers something to Arianna and points at me. I tell myself I don't care. Arianna stares back. I smile grand and give a beauty-queen wave. I won. I'm moving on. My plan's working. *84, 88.* The duo turns away and says something to Bridgett. Gossip at full throttle. They're dissecting me like a formaldehyde frog. Bridgett tells them to shut up. I turn back around. Hannah's staring at me. No gossip, just kind eyes.

I want to feel happy, but the numbers crowd my head. *92, 96*. Only the numbers. *100, 104, 108, 112*. Ms. P. is talking logistics about the finals. I've stopped listening. I need to count. Can't lose my place.

I slide out a piece of clean, white, lined paper and sharpen an unused No. 2 to the perfect point and begin to write. The numbers start normal size, but then I write them smaller and smaller to squeeze more onto the page. *116, 120, 124, 128*. The worry retreats. It's working! As long as I count, nothing will hurt Ian. *132, 136*. I rotate the paper and begin to write the numbers up the right side of the paper. *140, 144*.

35

missing

"CLASS, THE FINAL ROUND starts in just a few minutes. Everyone put away your math books and backpacks. We leave for the auditorium shortly."

I neatly fold my paper in quarters, put it into my front pocket, and grab for my sea glass.

But it's not there.

I look again.

It's gone.

I check the floor.

Nothing.

My pockets.

Nothing.

Check my desk one more time. Still nothing. The numbers erupt in my brain. *4, 8, 12, 16, 20, 24, 28, 32.*

"Okay, class, let's head to the auditorium. Quiet in the halls, please," Ms. P. says as she shuttles everyone out of the room.

36, 40, 44, 48.

I don't move from my desk.

Ms. P. comes over. "Molly, time to go."

"Um, I just, um, need a minute. Can I meet you there?" I ask. *52, 56, 60, 64.*

"Sure, but don't be long. We can't start without you." She smiles.

I nod. A wave of panic-fear-nausea lands in my chest.

My mind ticks. *Where could it be?* I look around the room.

Search the bookshelf in the back of the room.

Books. And more books. And Gretta's sketch pad.

Look behind the cage where Tortoise, the classroom guinea pig, lives.

Nothing.

Peek in Tortoise's cage.

Nothing.

I stand in the middle of the room. *Come on. Think.*

Glimpse in the flowerpots along the windowsill.

Nothing.

Stick my head in the art supply cabinet.

Nothing.

Stare at the clock on the wall.

My time is up.

A tightness grips my chest and steals my breath. This is the first time I feel truly alone.

No Mom *and* no sea glass.

36

my numbers
are showing

WHEN I GET TO the auditorium, everyone is seated. There are two chairs in the middle of the stage. Sebastian, the other finalist, is already standing in front of the one on the left. Ms. P. waves me over. Sebastian smiles. "Hey, good luck."

68, 72. I nod. *76, 80.*

Sebastian sits and I can see he's wearing matching socks. I'm waiting for it to help.

It doesn't.

Hannah and Bridgett end up sitting next to each other. Clearly, assigned seating.

The numbers tick off at a steady pace until I see my dad standing in the back of the auditorium next to who I assume are Sebastian's mom and dad. I forgot this part.

The part where the parents of the finalists get invited to the winner's round. Mom didn't come. It's just Dad. He waves. I deflate. At that moment, I realize that my plan's a worthless failure. Even if I won the whole thing, she was *never* coming to the banquet. I thought she would come. I mean, that's what moms do. But as I stare out at my lone parent, I realize I was wrong. Kate was right. Mom left us. Mom left me. The numbers march to a faster beat as I wonder if Ian has malaria or typhoid or EEE. *84, 88, 92, 96, 100, 104.*

Sebastian delivers his slam poem. I don't listen, but I see his parents clapping wildly at the end. Almost everyone is up, snapping their fingers and stamping their feet. Bridgett remains seated, picking the black nail polish off her thumbs. I'm grateful for her rebellious dedication.

The noise is loud and the room is hot. *Don't forget the numbers.* I should be thinking about the poem, but I can't.

I don't have one.

Ms. P. hands me the microphone. It feels heavy and my hands are slippery. I cough. And continue counting in my head. *108, 112, 116, 120.* The ocean of eyes stares at me. I glare back, but it doesn't make them stop. I see my dad. He's waiting for me to make him proud. *124, 128.*

"Whenever you're ready," Ms. P. says, assuming my pause is from nerves or for effect.

I share the only thing I can.

In my head the numbers spill. 132, 136.
Crowding my every thought. 140, 144.
I am frozen in space, unable to move. 148, 152.
On the right, the right, always the right. 156, 160.
I line, I straighten, I tuck, I clean. 164, 168.
But it's not enough. 172, 176.
The numbers come, they flood, they pour. 180, 184.
No normal thoughts anymore. 188, 192.

I look out at the faces. My eyes reach Dad's and the numbers can no longer stay silent. They spill out of me.

"196, 200, 204, 208, 212, 216, 220, 224."

My numbers are showing. They're out in the open for everyone to see. They tick and tick and tick and tick.

"228, 232, 236, 240, 244, 248, 252, 256."

I can't stop.

37

behind the
velvet curtain

DEAD SILENCE FILLS THE room.

Ms. P. claps and scurries onstage, unsure of what just happened.

The eyes across the auditorium stick to me, then slowly I see Bridgett and Hannah stand and clap. I refuse to look at the back of the room. I can't handle the shock on Dad's face. The numbers scatter. Can't remember which one I'm on.

I run off and find a spot behind the thick velvet curtain where no one can see me. I grab the paper out of my pocket, pick a number, and count and count and count. *132, 136.* Finally, I'm alone with my numbers.

Breathe.

Ms. P. finds me. The heat in my body rises. I don't want her here. The sweat swims to the crook of my neck. Sticky. Hot. I speed up. *140, 144, 148, 152, 156, 160, 164, 168.*

I know if I look up at her she'll be staring at me, eyebrows raised, forehead shiny, head tilted, eyes intensely fixed on mine. *But I can't tell her. I can't tell anyone. Maybe Mom, but she's not here, not coming. 172, 176.*

"Molly." She bends down toward me. I feel her staring into the top of my head as my counting song crescendos.

180, 184, 188, 192.

A gentle hand rests on my shoulder. I flinch.

"It's all right. I promise you. Just look at me."

"I can't." *196, 200. Drip. Drip.* The salty wet trickles down my back.

They'll hate me.

I hate me. 204, 208.

"Molly, please talk to me."

Silence.

"Molly."

Silence.

Ms. P.'s hot breath blows toward me.

I nod and shift and bite my top lip. My eyes fall back on my paper. *212, 216.*

She reaches down and takes my paper.

Please don't take my numbers. DON'T TAKE AWAY MY NUMBERS!

Uneasiness marches up my calf. It's braver now. It knows I've lost my armor.

I find the dots in the tile and begin to count them.

Faster. Faster. Faster.

4, 8, 12, 16.

I wonder if there is the same number of dots in each tile. *20, 24.* Tiles one, two, and three all have sixty-eight.

"Molly, it's okay. You can talk to me."

I hear the stomp of the school emptying into the corridor. I stay hidden behind the curtain, but I hear Arianna's voice in the hallway. "So what's the deal with Molly? She's totally flipping out today." Her voice is like a slap across my face.

Ignore. Can't remember how many dots were in tile one.

"She doesn't feel well. It's no big deal," Hannah says.

"No big deal? She looks like the homeless lady who sleeps on the corner of Fourth and Ludlow downtown, and she, like, totally freaked out onstage," Arianna says.

Just count. What number was I on? 108, 112. I can't remember.

"Shut up!" Hannah defends. "She's fine. She's just sick. A flu or something. That's it."

116, 120. I wish I had paper. This doesn't feel right.

"Well, of course you're going to say that. She's your best friend. But heads up, your friend has lost it. You'll see, this is just the beginning."

"Arianna, don't be such an idiot. Molly's fine. I was with her all weekend. She has the flu," Bridgett says.

The flock goes quiet.

Thank you, B.

124, 128.

"Molly, please look at me," Ms. P. says, jarring me back to my spot behind the curtain.

I can't. If I look at you, you'll know my secret. 132, 136.

"I care about you, Molly, and I want to help."

"You can't," I whisper.

My concentration's slipping. *140, 144.* I feel a soft hand under my chin as she lifts my face and looks into my bloodshot eyes. The tears roll down my cheeks. "No one can help me. It's too late."

"It's never too late to get help."

148, 152, 156, 160.

"If I stop, bad things will happen."

"Stop what?" she asks, her voice like a soft blanket meant to keep me safe and warm.

"Counting," I whisper. Then I say the numbers aloud, "164, 168, 172, 176." My wounds are open now.

"Oh, Molly." She reaches out and hugs me.

38

there's a spot
on the floor

THE HALL'S QUIET AND empty except for Ms. P., my counting, and me.

4, 8, 12, 16. As we walk to Principal James's office, I reach into my pocket for my sea glass. But then I remember that it's gone. Like Mom.

I'm worried about Ian. *If Dad is here, who is with Ian? What if he stops breathing and no one's there to notice? What if he needs to go to the hospital and no one can drive him? 20, 24, 28, 32.* Yesterday, there was a story in the *Boston Globe* about a seven-year-old boy whose dad thought he had the flu. He tucked the boy in at bedtime and in the morning, the boy was dead. Some undiagnosed something.

If Ms. P. stops interrupting me, then I can keep him

safe. 36, 40, 44, 48. She doesn't get it. 52, 56, 60, 64. If I stop, I know bad things, awful things, will happen. That's what happened with Papa Lou when I didn't find the right spot on my shelf for Huey the raccoon. I can't let it happen again. Not with Ian. 68, 72, 76, 80.

I see Ms. P.'s mouth moving. I think she's trying to say something, but I don't hear her. I don't hear anything anymore. It's me, my numbers, and my fear. *84, 88, 92, 96.* She looks like she's in an old-time movie with no sound. Her hands are gently brushing the air in rhythm with her mouth as her eyes gaze at me like I am a battered lamb. *She doesn't get it. I'm only beaten when I have to stop. I don't have to stop. 100, 104, 108, 112. I never have to stop.*

116, 120, 124, 128.

We turn the corner into the principal's office. The hands of the clock finally creep toward 3:00 p.m. The bell sounds, and I wonder who's with the class since Ms. P. is with me.

I've never been to Principal James's office. *132, 136, 140, 144.* There are two metal chairs across from his ginormous desk. All of this year's class pictures hang on the walls, and next to his computer is a photograph of him with his wife and two children. *A perfect four.*

I have five in my family. It's not four and it's an odd number. 148, 152.

The office shares a waiting space with the health center, and as I look up, I can see Nurse Ramos bending down to wipe off Jessie Anne's bloody knee. *If only my crazy could be wiped off. 156, 160.* Then I see Hannah trying to get my attention from the hall. She waves. I don't. *164, 168.*

Ms. P. motions for me to sit down and Principal James smiles at me. *172, 176. I can't let him distract me. The worry is beginning to retreat. A calm's coming. Ian will be okay.* The principal's lips move. I drop my head down and focus on the numbers. *180, 184, 188, 192.* I notice a spot on the office floor. My insides turn. *Leave it. It's not your mess to clean. 196, 200, 204, 208.* I close my eyes. I don't see the spot anymore. *212, 216.*

My silence comes to a crashing halt when the door to the office flies open.

It's Dad.

39

the death of
spider-man

THE NUMBERS TUMBLE AND fall. They can't shield me from the worry in my dad's eyes. I'm not sick. Just crazy. And lost. Like my numbers.

"Molly, it's okay. I'm here," Dad says. His eyes are kind and filled with concern.

And confusion.

"I've been looking for you. I was, um, worried after your poem."

"Who's with Ian? Is he okay?" My mind races to the worst place. Dad has really come to tell me Ian's dead at home in his little bed in his Spider-Man pajamas. I scramble to remember my numbers. I need them. I grab the ones that find my brain first. *240, 244.*

He reaches for my hand. "Ian's fine. Aunt Lucy is with

him. In fact, she's in the kitchen right now making him some of her famous pea soup." He says it to make me laugh because Aunt Lucy's a terrible cook.

But I don't laugh. I count. *248, 252.*

He leans over and whispers, "Mol, tell me what's going on."

I say nothing.

Dad looks over at Principal James and Ms. P. "Will someone tell me what's going on?"

256, 260. Just keep counting. Ignore them. Don't stop. 264, 268, 272, 276.

"Mol, what happened up there?"

I sit silently and count. *280, 284.*

"While I'm not a doctor, it's my belief your daughter may be suffering from anxiety or severe stress," says Ms. P.

288, 292, 296, 300.

Dad drops his head into his big hands and is quiet for a very long minute. "A while back, my wife left to live in Toronto for a year. I work a lot. It's been hard on Molly." When he looks over at me this time, tears roll down his cheeks. He reaches over and brushes my hair away from my eyes.

304, 308.

"I think this is the fallout from all of that. I know she's upset, but I think she's all right." He turns to me, "Mol, what do you think?"

First, nothing. Then, slowly and so quietly that Principal James has to lean over his desk to hear me, I say, "Yep, I'm fine."

Dad exhales, stands, and heads toward the door.

"Molly, what did you say after the word *fine*? I couldn't hear you," Ms. P. says. "It's okay, Molly, you can tell us." Her gentle voice is like a life jacket in a storm.

"312, 316, 320, 324, 328, 332."

Dad turns back.

"336, 340, 344, 348."

"Mr. Nathans, we believe that your daughter may need to talk to someone. We have a school counselor on hand if you'd like to speak with her. Otherwise, you can certainly pursue this on your own."

352, 356, 360, 364, 368, 372.

"I appreciate your concern, but I honestly think Molly's just upset about her mom relocating. Even though it's just for a year," my dad explains to Principal James and Ms. P. "I think it's best if I take her home and she and I have a chance to talk about things." He starts toward the door again.

This time I follow him out of the principal's office. *376, 380, 384, 388.*

I glance back at Ms. P. She looks at me the way I used to look at Hannah when the kids in third grade teased her that her gym uniform was too tight. I want to stay with Ms. P. She doesn't care that I count. She doesn't care that I'm crazy.

I stare at the floor as I shuffle one foot in front of the other behind the Pied Piper. *392, 396.* I make sure to keep the numbers tucked in my head. No sharing.

When I move into the front seat of the car, I feel like I'm going to suffocate. I crack the window and pray. My scab itches. I scratch it. The blood trickles onto my sock. *Socks. I hate them.* I cross my ankles. Hidden sores. The heat moves up my legs into my body. I count faster. *400, 404, 408, 412.*

We don't speak the entire ride home. The numbers fill my head. When we pull into our driveway, I've made it to 600. A beautiful number. Dad turns off the car. The silence is loud. "Mol, we need to talk." He looks at me. "What's wrong?"

I'm crazy.

"Please answer me," he begs in a hushed tone.

"I don't know." *604, 608.*

"I know it's been hard without Mom here. I'm sorry."
He looks out the window.

612, 616, 620, 624.

The tears make it hard to concentrate.

He hates me.

"We'll spend more time together. I'll take Fridays off."

I look at him. I have to ask. "Did Mom know?"

"Know what?"

"About the final round. Being invited. Did she know?"

Dad looks away.

"Tell me."

"Honey, she couldn't come. It was short notice and she had some presentation at the Juice Convention."

The air in my lungs shrinks.

"I'm sorry, Mol. I love you."

Before he can begin again, I open the car door, bolt into the house, run up the stairs, slam my door, and dive onto my bed.

628, 632, 636, 640.

Just me, my numbers, and B. B. King. Until I look over at my glass animal collection.

"Ian!" I scream.

40

the power of
the band-aid

THE NUMBERS SCATTER IN my brain like pick-up sticks.

"Ian!" I yell again. Anger and worry compete for my attention. *644, 648, 652, 656.* My glass figurines are crooked, cock-eyed, knocked over. *Everything* is out of order.

B. B. King's beat interrupts my thoughts to remind me there were supposed to be twenty-five days until Mom's first visit. I throw my phone across the room. My plan would have never worked. She was never coming home. Kate was right.

The tears pour down my face. I think of the slam. Now everyone knows I'm crazy. Everyone hates me. *I* hate me. Breathing is hard and choppy and just hard. I think about Mom. I hate her. She didn't come. She was never coming. Even if I won the whole stupid thing, she was never coming to my banquet. She was never coming back to Ian, to Kate, to me. I thought I could fix things. But I can't.

I pick up Huey the raccoon. *660, 664.* I hate these stupid figurines. *668, 672.* Going to something *is* exactly the same as leaving. It's tiring to think and count and breathe. Before I can stop myself, I take Huey and stomp him with the heel of my boot. Then again. And again. And again. Small brown bits of glass shatter under my foot. *676, 680.* I grab Harry the horse, the cow, the piglet, the eagle. I swipe my arm across my dresser and knock the rest of my figurines onto the floor. None are safe from the bottom of my boot.

Stomp and *stomp* and *stomp* and *stomp.*

Mom isn't coming home. I can't find perfect anymore. 684, 688. It's lost. Like me.

When I'm done, I sit and cry. *692, 696.*

Ian walks in mid-knock. He says, "I'm sorry. I know I wasn't allowed to . . . ," but stops talking when he sees me sobbing in a pile of smashed glass.

"Nothing's where it's supposed to be. Where it *needs* to be," I say. The numbers are lost. I begin again. *4, 8, 12, 16.*

"Molly, I tried to put everything back the way it was,

but I couldn't remember where the elephant went. Then I, um, I, um, accidentally broke the dolphin." He picks at the skin around his thumbnail. "I'm really, really sorry."

My body screams on the inside, but I'm quiet. *20, 24.*

"Molly," his little voice says, "you're bleeding." Ian points to my ankle.

"I'm bleeding because I was worried you were lying dead on the couch." *28, 32.*

He scrunches up his nose and takes a step back.

"I was worried you were dead because I lost my lucky sea glass and you messed up my stuff and I broke it all into tiny pieces because I couldn't stand any of it anymore!" My face feels like it's on fire.

Ian ignores my rant. "What did you think I died from?" He innocently looks around my room for any sign of impending doom.

I bite the inside of my cheek and apologize to Ian a thousand times in my head. *36, 40.*

"I'll get you a Band-Aid." He flies out of my room.

"I don't want a Band-Aid. Just leave me alone," I say to the empty air. *60. Is that right? What number am I on? Think. Count. Think. What number? I don't remember. Ugh! I have to start again. 4, 8.*

"Here you go," he says, sweeping back into my room,

his feet faster than his body. He holds out a small tan Band-Aid as if that can fix me.

"I don't need that stupid thing. It's not going to do anything!"

12, 16, 20, 24.

"Yes, it will. It'll take away the blood so it doesn't get on your floor."

He's so sweet and little and deserves a better sister than me. "I don't care about my stupid carpet." As I say the words, I know they're not true. The blood spots on the floor will haunt my perfect world even as it crumbles around me.

28, 32, 36, 40.

"I know you like things neat. Real neat. That's why you wash your hands all the time." He reaches deep into his pocket and pulls out a fistful of Band-Aids. "Here, take them all. They'll make you better."

"Better! Are you kidding? A Band-Aid can't fix me!" I pause for a moment. *Am I ready to say it out loud?* *44, 48, 52, 56.*

"I'm crazy, Ian. Not hurt, just nuts."

My whole body stiffens. *There, it's out. I said it.* I stare at Ian and feel his sad eyes seeing straight into the part of me that can't hide, the part that hurts, the part that's really me. *60, 64.*

I wait for him to say something.

But he doesn't.

He looks at me with his big ocean eyes and gives me an all-his-might hug. Then he opens his tiny hand and sitting in his palm is my sea glass.

"I borrowed it. We had to climb across the monkey bars in gym class and I didn't know if I could do it. You always say your sea glass is lucky, so I, um, took it. But only for today."

Then he drops the sea glass, the taped-together dolphin, the Band-Aids, and runs out of my room.

I pick up my special sea glass, spin it in my hands, and then throw it against the wall. Tiny turquoise pieces rain down on my orange carpet.

41

shattered glass

THE DOORBELL RINGS. I haven't left my room since my confession to Ian. I told someone. I said it. Out loud. I'm crazy. Really. My fingers tingle. My breath feels small, too small. The glass hurts my knees, but I don't move. The numbers are like a word scramble. Counting's impossible. I look down and see the Band-Aid on my ankle and the droplets of blood on my carpet. I don't recognize the person looking back at me in the mirror. *Where have I gone?*

I hear Ian yell from downstairs. "Molly, Hannah and Bridgett are here!"

Hannah and Bridgett. Together?

I take a deep breath. The numbers begin again. *4, 8, 12, 16.*

Knock. Knock.

The door is ajar.

"Mol, it's us. Me and Bridgett. Can we come in?" Hannah asks in a soft voice.

Nothing.

"Mol, we just want to drop off your backpack." She gently pushes the door open even more. First, I see Hannah's reflection in the mirror. It takes her a minute to realize the person looking back at her is me. I don't look like me. Not really.

She wedges herself through the door, followed closely by Bridgett.

"Hey," Hannah says. She takes in the broken glass, lays down her jacket, sits down next to me, and holds my hand. I want to pull my hand away. *20, 24, 28, 32.* But I don't. My anger at Hannah, and everyone, left with my confession. Bridgett sits on my other side.

An uncomfortable silence settles in.

"I like your mashed potatoes." Hannah tries to make me laugh. She and Bridgett giggle nervously.

Hannah tries again. "It's going to be okay." She brushes my ratty hair away from my face and holds out her pinky. Bridgett's still like stone.

"I don't think so," I say. *36, 40.* "This time we can't fix things with our pinky shake."

"No one cares about the stupid slam contest," Bridgett offers.

44, 48.

"It doesn't matter. It's not about that. I just can't be fixed." *52, 56, 60, 64.*

"Mol, don't say that," Hannah says. "You were amazing in Round Two. You just had a bad day; you're not broken."

"Like in today's obits, Mr. Cavanaugh died when an old guy accidentally stepped on the gas instead of the brake and ran poor Mr. Cavanaugh over while he was buying cough medicine at the convenience store. They both had really bad days."

Hannah gives her a you're-not-helping look. "E. B. Rule Number 19: Failure is just opportunity's way of telling you to be more creative." Hannah gives my hand a little squeeze.

"No. It's not. Failure is just failure. You don't know because you're perfect." *68, 72.*

"Uh, don't think so. My hair isn't brushed most days. My clothes consist of many different shades of brown. I'm terrible in science and . . ."

"Hannah, your name has six letters. An even number. Not divisible by four, but still very good. And it's the same backward and forward. Bridgett, your name has eight letters. Also even *and* divisible by four. My name has five letters. Odd. Awful." *76, 80.*

"Mol, I don't get it. You're the perfect one. Really. You have the best hair. Mac, Ryan, and I'm pretty sure Greg all have crushes on you. You get good grades and—"

"None of that matters." *84, 88, 92, 96.*

"Why not?" Hannah chews her top lip the way she does when she's confused.

"Because I'm, I'm . . ."

Just say it.

"You're what? Please tell me—us. We want to help," Hannah pleads.

"I'm crazy." *100, 104.*

There.

"Molly, you're not crazy, you're just stressed. You've had a lot to deal with. I mean, with your mom moving to Canada and your dad working so much, it happens," Hannah says. "We all do weird stuff when we're stressed."

Bridgett chimes in. "Look, I told you that thing about my dad." She looks at Hannah, not wanting to say too much. "Now, I read the obits every day. Stress makes us do things we wouldn't normally do. It's okay."

I stand up, place my hands on my friends' shoulders

and look into their faces for the first time in months. "No, I really am crazy." There's no stopping me now. "The slam was just part of it. I've been counting by four under my breath since you walked into the room. I can only have someone walk on my right side, the left is bad—always. I brush my hair and my teeth in sections four times each and if I'm not sure I did it right, I need to start all over again. I wash my hands so much they're cracking. My glass animals need to be aligned with my ruler. My homework's done sometimes four times until it's finished with no mistakes, smudges, or eraser marks. Each morning, I sharpen and organize my pencils. I could go on, but by the look on your faces, I think you get the picture." *108, 112.*

"Mol, when?" Hannah twirls some strands of her blue tips around her pointer finger and looks from me to Bridgett, then back to me.

"For a while."

"Why?"

"To keep bad things from happening." *116, 120.*

"To who?" Bridgett says.

"Ian. When I stop counting, washing, or whatever stupid thing I need to do to feel right, the worry explodes in my head and won't leave me alone. Ian's sick. Ian's hurt. Ian's dead. The worry never leaves." *124, 128, 132, 136.*

"Oh, Molly." Hannah hugs me. Bridgett hugs me.

They love me anyway.

42

just like grammy jean

DAD WALKS IN. HE stops for a moment, as his eyes sweep across my carpet now covered with broken pieces of colored glass. Then he makes that big inhale noise he makes when he has bad news to share. The last time he did it was when Mom left for Toronto. "Girls, Molly and I need to talk. This may be a good time to head home. You can certainly come back and visit later."

"No, Dad, they can stay. I want them to stay." *140, 144.*

He finds a place on the edge of my bed, takes a big gulp of his water, and sits down. "I just got off the phone with your mother."

My eyes brim and tiny tears streak my cheeks. I miss her. *148, 152.*

"I told her what happened today."

Here comes the bad news. "She's never coming back, is she?"

"What?" My dad looks startled. "Mol, of course she's coming home."

"But I thought when I didn't see her at the finals, she forgot about us and decided to stay in Toronto. Forever."

Dad wipes my tears and brushes the hair from my eyes. "Your mom and I both love you. She went *to* a job in Toronto, not *away* from you, Kate, and Ian. There's a difference."

"It doesn't feel different."

"I know," Dad says. "But that doesn't matter anymore. She's leaving Toronto."

"For good?" I pluck a glass piece of the eagle's broken wing from the carpet.

"Not sure. One day at a time. But when we spoke, she shared something that I never knew."

"I didn't think you guys had secrets."

"We don't. This wasn't a secret. Just something that happened before I knew your mom. It has to do with your Grammy Jean, who died before Mom and I even dated. When I explained to Mom what had been going on, she told me that she and Aunt Lucy thought Grammy had Obsessive-Compulsive Disorder."

The numbers pick up pace. *156, 160.* My gaze drops to the glass-flecked carpet. Now I know the bad news. Hannah puts her arm around me.

"Back then, there was no official diagnosis, but from what Mom described, it sounds a lot like OCD."

"What does that mean exactly?" Hannah asks, but I already know the answer. Maybe I knew all along.

"OCD is when you have unwanted thoughts you can't get rid of." Dad scratches his goatee and takes a sip of his water. "And to try and make the unwelcome ideas go away, you sometimes do unrelated stuff over and over again."

"Like what?" Bridgett asks.

Again, I say nothing. But I know what the unrelated stuff is. Counting. Organizing. Brushing. Cleaning. The list is too long and too stupid to say out loud. *164, 168.*

"Molly's mom said Grammy washed her hands until they bled because she was afraid if she didn't she'd spread germs that would contaminate and kill all the people she loved."

"She knew, I mean really knew, she wasn't going to

kill off her family because she didn't wash her hands before dinner. Right?" Bridgett asks.

"Yes and no. I guess she knew her fear was irrational, but it didn't matter."

I stare into the mirror across the room. *Everyone says I have Grammy's gold-flecked eyes. Am I like her?* I look at my own hands. *172, 176.*

"What happened to her?" I hear myself ask.

"I guess at first she didn't tell anyone. She was just a kid; she thought she was going crazy." I look at my dad and wonder if he wishes he had a different kid. "One day she refused to leave the house. She insisted that her hands were dirty. She'd wash them, touch something, anything—a chair, a doorknob, a wall—and then feel like they were contaminated again."

I sit on my hands.

"She'd run back to the bathroom and scrub them. After hours of this, your great-grandmother finally called the doctor. When she brought Grammy in to talk with him, her hands were bleeding. She had washed the skin right off."

The room is quiet.

"Back then, there were no doctors that specialized in OCD for kids," Dad says.

"Other kids have it, too?" Bridgett asks.

"Millions of kids."

Hannah chews on the side of her nail. "What does this have to do with Molly?" Hannah asks.

"It's hereditary."

43

can i catch it?

WHEN DAD LEAVES MY room, Bridgett, Hannah, and I let the silence sink in. The numbers skip. *192, 196.* My brain is tired.

Then Bridgett says, "I worry about lots of stuff. Maybe I have it, too."

Hannah says, "Maybe. But we don't even *know* if Molly has it. And everyone worries and does stuff to feel better. Like I keep my closet light on all night and wear my lucky pink tee every time I take a test." She pauses. "That's why pop quizzes can be tricky."

"Can I catch it? You know, am I going to wake up tomorrow and start organizing my obits alphabetically by last name?" Bridgett asks.

Hannah kicks Bridgett.

"No offense," Bridgett says.

200, 204.

Bridgett opens her laptop and plugs Obsessive-Compulsive Disorder into SearchMaster. I already know the site that will pop up. She clicks on the website for the OCD Foundation.

"I can't believe there are so many people who have this thing that there's an entire organization for it," Bridgett says.

208, 212.

"Okay, it says here that OCD is not contagious," Hannah explains. "So can you stop freaking out and close that thing?" Hannah points to B's computer.

"No. Listen to this." Bridgett reads from the site. "Max, age thirteen, says his worry is like a broken faucet that won't shut off. His parents have to reassure him over and over again he hasn't hurt anyone's feelings and nothing bad is about to happen. His anxiety got so overwhelming he wouldn't go to school for fear that something awful would happen."

"Bridgett, stop," Hannah grunts.

B ignores her and reads on. "Miranda, age eleven, is a checker. She checks everything she does ten times just to make sure she's really done it. George, age twelve, is like Grammy Jean, the classic germ-o-phobe—washing his hands until they bleed. It says each kid has a worry they can't turn off. Just like a broken faucet."

216, 220.

Hannah gives her one last kick in the shin.

Lots of broken faucets.

44

panic rising

MY RELIEF-ANXIETY BLEND WASHES away like warm bath-water. Everyone knows my secret. *456, 460.* No more hiding.

Dad comes back into my room after Hannah and Bridgett leave. Gingerly, he finds a seat next to me on my bed.

"I promise you that we'll figure out what's happening. Maybe it's OCD, maybe it's something else. Either way, you're not alone." He lifts my trembling chin and kisses my forehead. "I'm sorry. I feel like this is my fault. I've been working so much. I haven't been there for you. I get it. You need me and I'm going to be here for you. You don't have to do this stuff anymore."

"Dad, it's not your fault. You didn't *do* this." I stare out my bedroom window into our once-manicured, now-overgrown backyard. The weeds are like the weird things I do—overpowering and relentless. "You don't understand. This has nothing to do with you. I can't stop. My mind won't let me. This is the only way to protect Ian." *464, 468.* I think back to Maria F. on Facebook and remember that she washes her hands to protect her little brother. I hope she avoids odd numbers.

"Protect him from what?" Dad stands up, his hands cutting the air as he speaks.

"Bad things." *472, 476.*

"Mol, what does that mean?"

"I don't know. I just know how it feels. It feels like I'm gone. The Molly I used to be has been replaced by a crazy person."

"You're not gone. You're still my Molly. We'll figure this out."

Breathe.

"I'm going to call Dr. Andrews," Dad says as he leaves my room.

Kate pokes her head in. "So, rough day at the slam?"

"I don't want to talk about it." *480, 484, 488, 492.*

Kate's truly perfect. Four letters in her name, five feet four inches tall. She gets straight A's, is a star soccer player for her high school, and has great hair.

"I get it." She walks in and sits down next to me, putting her arm around me. "You're going to be all right."

"How do you know?"

"Because you're my sister."

I lean my head against her shoulder. *496, 500.*

45

the wrong spot

"IT'S TIME," DAD YELLS from the bottom of the steps.

"Now?" Panic rises from behind my belly button.

"Yes, now. Our appointment with Dr. Andrews is in fifteen minutes. I need to grab my keys. Meet me downstairs."

My sister gives me a hug and leaves me to my own fears.

I look around my room at the remnants of yesterday's crash-and-burn session. Broken pieces of colored figurines, scraps of turquoise sea glass, and lots of scattered Band-Aids. My stomach tightens. I kneel down to pull the larger pieces of Huey and Harry from my shag carpet. I reach for a piece of the panda's back foot.

"Molly!" Dad's footsteps are getting closer. My throat

tightens and the sweat trickles slowly around my ear, down the side of my neck. He steps into my room. "We need to leave."

"I can't. I have to . . ."

"You have to come with me. That's what you have to do."

"I can't. I have to fix my room before I leave or it won't be right. Nothing will be right." I'm crying. It's too much—the worry, the perfection, the counting.

In a soft but firm voice, Dad says, "Mol, you need to get up now and come with me." He helps me stand. He looks me in the eye. "I love you, but I can't do this alone. We need to do this together." Pause. "Please. We have to go."

I hold his hand and follow him out of my room. He closes the door. My unkempt room screams at me. I trudge down the stairs and lose count. *Have to start over. 4, 8, 12, 16. Room's a mess. 20, 24, 28, 32.* I'm dizzy. My fingers tingle. It's hard to breathe.

When we finally get to the pediatrician's office, the panda's broken foot is still in my hand. I push up my glasses. The rhythm of the clock's tick keeps the beat of my counting. *104 tick 108 tick 112 tick 116 tick.* I close my eyes. Exhaustion floods my body. I lean my head against Dad's shoulder. He leans in and kisses my forehead.

"It's going to be all right," he whispers.

120 tick 124 tick 128 tick 132 tick. I wish I believed him. I open my eyes. I notice the boy across the room staring at me. *Can he tell what's wrong with me?*

136 tick 140 tick.

The blond curls on the little girl next to me bounce as she twirls. Thirteen times. Then she shoves her left pointer finger up her button nose, pulls out a booger, and pops it into her mouth.

A burning rises in my throat. *144 tick 148 tick 152 tick 156 tick.*

"Molly Nathans," calls the gangly woman holding my manila folder.

Dad and I follow the nurse to Dr. Andrews's office, where he's waiting for us.

"Hello, Mr. Nathans." He shakes my dad's hand. "Molly." He nods and then lowers his large bottom into his black, fake-leather chair. I sit in the chair on the right.

"So, Molly, why don't you tell me what's going on?" His voice is gentle.

160, 164, 168, 172.

"Dr. Andrews, I'm very worried about Molly." Dad turns to look at me, almost apologetically. "Um. She says she's counting all the time, going on about keeping things neat and bad things happening to her little brother. It's important to know that my wife and I recently separated and then she relocated to Toronto for the year. And, well, I told Molly we'd spend more time together, but—"

"Mr. Nathans, I appreciate your concern, but I need to hear from Molly. In fact, it might be a good idea for me to speak with Molly privately and then you can join us at the end."

My dad looks over. He doesn't want to abandon me.

I nod.

He rises and slowly heads to the door. "Mol, I'll be in the waiting room if you need me." He exits.

Relief.

"Now, Molly, can you share with me why you're here?" Dr. Andrews leans back in his chair and folds his hands behind his head. I wonder if he likes the number four.

For a moment, I stare at the floor, trying to remember what number I am on. The worry is exposed. *I need to find that number. 176* (That's it!), *180, 184, 188.* Then I tell the doctor about every crazy thought I've ever had and weird thing I've ever done.

"The first time I remember feeling anything strange

was the day Papa Lou died. When he gave me Huey, Nana Rose's special glass raccoon figurine, and told me to put him in the perfect spot in my room. Then he died. I think I put Huey in the wrong spot." I look up at the doctor. He's listening with his hands interlocked behind his gray, thinning hair. *192, 196.*

I take a deep breath and wipe away my tears.

"Molly, what's perfect? What does it look like? Feel like?" he asks.

"Aligned. Equal. Even. So I measure the figurines. Once, twice, three times, four times. Until they feel right. That's what perfection is, really. When everything just feels right." *200, 204.*

"How does it feel now?" He writes something on the lined paper in front of him.

"Awful. Wrong. I can't find perfect anymore. It takes too long. There's too much stuff my brain says I have to do to feel just right. At first it was just keeping things neat, then the number four came into it—don't ask me why—then brushing my hair, picking out my clothes, getting dressed, undressed, doing my schoolwork, walking." *208, 212.*

"It must be hard for you." He looks into my eyes over his glasses. They're round and black like mine.

"It was hard, but not impossible until the worry came. When it came, things got ugly and weird. Weirder." *216, 220.*

"Tell me about the worry."

I search for ridicule in his words, but there is none. He just listens to me. Really.

"I worry about my brother, Ian. If I don't do all the stupid stuff I need to do to make me feel okay, bad things will happen to him." I scratch my scab and it opens again. Blood starts to trickle down my leg. *224, 228.*

"What kind of bad things?"

"Like he's going to die in his sleep or from Triple E or get hit by our neighbor driving to work." *232, 236.*

He says nothing.

I look up at him. I have to know. "Do you think I'm crazy?" My voice trembles with the possibility that I am.

46

weird for a reason

MY DAD ENTERS DR. Andrews's office, worry etched into
the wrinkles on his forehead.

A burning sensation churns in my stomach.

"I believe your daughter has what her grandmother
likely had: Obsessive-Compulsive Disorder."

240, 244, 248, 252.

He says more, but all I can think about is Parker Ray
and Maria F.

When we get home, I run straight to my room. I
close my eyes tightly and wish hard for a different me.
A me that doesn't care about perfection or counting or
the number four. I try to remember a me before *this*
me came along. I can see her, barely. The counting resets.
4, 8, 12, 16. I guess if I made my OCD list now, I'd have

more yeses. Maybe it was always that way, but I just didn't see it.

My phone rings. It's Mom.

The minute I hear her voice, the tears roll with purpose. "Hey, Mol."

"Hi."

"It's going to be all right." The sound of her voice makes me almost believe her.

I nod, but say nothing, forgetting she can't see me.

"I love you, Mol. I'm coming back." I should be happy. This is what I wanted. But now, I'm just numb. I hang up the phone and look around my room. My snowy white dresser is bare for the first time since Papa Lou handed me Huey in the Rockville Diner. The kaleidoscope of smashed glass on my floor is completely gone.

"Hey, how'd we do?" It's numbers one and three—Kate and Ian.

"Good. Thanks." I'm touched they tried to clean up my mess. *20, 24.*

"Dad said Mom's coming home," Kate says.

"I know."

"So, maybe you're weird for a reason. She should be here. She should have never left." Kate and I share a silent understanding.

"You know you smell like her," she says.

I hug my sister as I count in my head. *28, 32, 36, 40.*

Ian's standing at my desk in his Spider-Man costume.

"Hey, Buddy, I'm sorry that I yelled at you," I say. "You didn't do anything wrong. Okay?"

"Okay," he says, then sticks out his hand and gives me Beethoven the Zebra. "Kate helped me glue it back together."

47

welcome home

THE NEXT DAY, MOM'S in the kitchen when I come into the house after a walk with Oscar. She's wearing our brown birthday boots. Her black hair is still short. I run my hands through my twenty-six inches.

"You lied," I say to the back of her cranberry sweater. This isn't how I imagined our reunion. I envisioned hugs and tears and I-love-yous. But instead, these words spill out onto the tile floor.

She spins around and steps closer with the hug I've desperately wanted.

I move back. The numbers spit. *20, 24, 28, 32.* "You said you weren't *leaving* me, but *going* to something. That was a lie."

She sets her glass of water on the whipped-crème

white Formica table. "It wasn't. I meant it. I went to Toronto for work. I didn't leave you."

36, 40, 44, 48. "But you did. You left me and Kate and Ian. And Dad."

She looks away. She can't deny the last one. They'd been separated for six months before her escape to Toronto.

I stare at her newly painted nails. Blue like Hannah's bangs. She never used to wear nail polish.

She steps in. *52, 56, 60, 64.* I step back.

"I'm sorry, Mol. I am."

My reminder ring goes off. Mom smiles.

"I didn't handle things well, but I'm back now."

I fight the tears that won't be ignored and leave her standing alone in the kitchen.

In my room, I find what I'm looking for and am about to head downstairs when I hear the kitchen door open and slam close.

Then Mom's boots walking toward the door.

Then Kate's voice. "Don't."

"I'm so happy to see you. I've missed you."

"Mom, don't," Kate warns.

"You look great."

"Seriously, don't."

"Don't what?"

"Don't act like you're my mom."

"But I am."

"You lost the right to parent me when you got on that plane to Toronto."

"Kate, that's not fair. I didn't abandon you. Dad was here."

"But *you* weren't. You weren't here when Kevin broke up with me. You weren't here when Ian cried himself to sleep every night. You weren't here when Molly came apart onstage in front of the entire school."

My body tightens at the mention of me and my unraveling. *68, 72.*

"So, yeah, you lost the right to try and parent me now," Kate says.

I can hear her crying and want Mom to say it's all going to be okay.

But she doesn't.

When I get back to the kitchen, I see Ian hugging Mom, and Kate standing on the other side of the room with a box of tissues.

I walk over to Mom and hand her the beaded necklaces. Then I stand by Kate.

Mom's face confirms what Kate told me.

She left them. She left us. She left me. *76, 80.*

Mom drapes the necklaces around her neck. "Thank you," she says. "I've missed these. I've missed all of you. I know there's no way to explain this to you three, but when I left, I needed to go. But now, the only place I need to be is here with you."

48

twizzler test

IT'S BEEN FOUR MONTHS and three days since *that* day on-stage.

I grab a magazine, pretend to read about some kid who solved the Rubik's Cube in a little over five seconds, and focus on not counting. I notice Dad staring at the shiny plaque on the wall that reads, *Don't let the perfect be the enemy of the good.—Anonymous.* Dr. Gretchen Gordon's office has stuff like that all around. In the bathroom it says, *I'm a person who also happens to have OCD.—Patricia Perkins-Doyle.* Dr. G. is the best referral I ever got from Dr. Andrews, even though her large rhinestone owl earrings took some getting used to.

The door to the office opens. Short spiky red hair walks in. It's Parker Ray. Turns out he lives just two towns over from me. We met last week in the waiting room and had a long talk about the number eleven. Still hard to believe that number makes anyone feel better. I wave.

"Hi," he says, sitting next to me.

"Hey."

Dad tries hard to act like he's not listening.

Parker tears open a bag of M&M's and pulls out the green ones. "There's this group of kids like us that meets Thursdays at the YMCA. Want to come?"

Before I can answer, a twenty-something in pastel pink calls, "Molly Nathans."

"I'll, um, let you know."

A group of kids like us. It's hard to imagine being in a room full of people who might like the number eleven. Parker Ray is the only one I've ever met. He has a beagle named Max, and last week we walked Max and Oscar around the block. Three times. Part of Dr. G.'s master plan.

I follow the nurse into Dr. G.'s office. The first time I was here, I confessed all of my weird stuff. Dr. G. didn't even flinch. She said that she's seen lots of kids do tons of weird stuff because they "have" to.

"My patients kiss windows, lick shoes, eat paper, tap

the light switch, read backward, and whistle four short times followed by one long one. Molly, you're not odd or crazy, you're just in need of some help," she had told me.

All I could think of was why anyone would want to lick a shoe.

"OCD is the doubting disease." Then she looked into that place inside me that most people don't see and said, "It's okay to be scared, but you don't have to be the victim of your brain. I'm going to give you what you need to fight the doubt and win. It'll be hard at first, but eventually it'll get easier." Then she handed me Twizzlers.

When I walk into her office today, the Twizzlers are on the table. There are ten. It's a test: I need to eat three. She talks to me while I grab the first one. "How did it go this past week at home?"

"I did okay yesterday and today. The first few days of the week were more like a C minus."

She shares a gentle smile. "Bright side, Molly. Remember, focus on the good stuff."

My homework last week—no counting. A month ago, I wasn't allowed to count by fours in class. Now I'm not supposed to count at all. This has been really hard. Really hard. She hands me another Twizzler.

"What about the glass animals?" She warned me this may be a tough one to break. I needed to ask Ian to play with them and then I could clean them up, but no ruler. After my freak-out-smash-and-trash, I only have fourteen left. Last week, I confessed that while I let Ian go all ninja on my glass figurines, I did use my ruler at the end. Just once.

"I'd say I'm a solid B, maybe even a B plus. I let Ian play with them and I even left the room." She slid the third Twizzler toward me. If I eat this one, there will be seven left.

"Where did you go?"

"My mom had stopped by."

Her eyebrow arch screams, *Well, isn't this interesting?* "How was that?"

"Fine." She stares at me an extra-long second. "I guess I'm more happy that she's back than mad that she left. Kate's still super mad. And Ian's just happy Mom can take him to school again." I pause, then add, "She was still wearing the beaded necklaces even though they completely clashed with her shirt, and she wanted me to try her new juice."

"Any good?"

"Better than the liquid salad, but worse than a

milkshake." Mom has kept her word and hasn't gone back to Toronto. She decided to start her own juice company, Mama's Juice, right here in Lantern. She said she wants to be around more.

"Have you visited her at her new apartment?" That was another part of my homework. I needed to spend time at Mom's new place. It's just two miles away from my real home, but Dr. G. knows that perfect doesn't travel well.

I nod and stare at the last Twizzler. "Last week, I went with Ian. We helped my mom blend the spinach, kale, leeks, and celery combination she's named Winter Rejuvenation. Then we left."

Before Dr. G. could quiz me about what I did and didn't do while I was there, I blurt out the latest romance news. "Mom and Dad went on a date." I know she loves this kind of stuff. *People* magazine and *Us Weekly* are all over her office.

High eyebrow arch this time.

"Last week, they went to The Flying Fish and came home past midnight. Kate and I waited up. We saw them laughing." That was date number two.

Dr. G. gives me a polite smile.

"I know it doesn't mean anything. Kate already warned

me. Anyway, I don't even know what I want to happen. For now, things are a step above fine."

"A step above fine sounds pretty good." A real smile. "We got off track. So what did the figurines look like when you returned to your room?"

"No big deal."

We both laugh.

"I cleaned them up. No ruler. No line. Just off the floor and onto my dresser." I eat the third Twizzler.

"I'm really proud of you."

"All this stuff makes me want to take a nap."

"I know, but it's working."

We talk about Ian and Kate and more about Mom and Dad. Then I ask her about what Parker Ray said. Dr. G. tells me there's a support group of kids with OCD and she thinks I should give it a try.

"Is it homework?"

She laughs. "No. It's a choice."

When our hour is almost over, she gives me my to-dos for next week. "I want you to mess up the collection yourself." She trails on with more directions, but I'm stuck on "mess up."

There is only one person who can help me with this assignment.

49

meet max

DAD HANDS ME SOME papers to proofread. That's my job today. He hates grammar and spelling. A few weeks ago, we decided to write an article together on children and OCD. In addition to all things grammar, I was in charge of the interviews. I interviewed Dr. G., Mom, Dad, Kate, Ian, and Parker Ray.

I am six hundred words in when Bridgett shows up. She hands me a very large black binder that says *Promising Obituaries* across the front. "I wrote these, and since you're all into this editing stuff, I thought you could edit this."

"What is it?"

"It's my book. I'm going to self-publish, but first I want to be sure everything's spelled correctly and there are no major mistakes. A grammar mistake in an obit would be totally embarrassing."

"When did you do all of this?" The book is at least three inches thick.

"I don't know. Over time. That's not the point. Will you edit it for me?"

"Sure, as soon as I'm done revising the article with my dad."

"Thanks. I'll leave it here with you. I've got another binder I can use while you work on this one. Oh, and if you ever need to write my obit, you should use these as a guide, especially Ms. Pinkman's on page seventy-six. It makes me cry every time I read it."

"B, we really need to find you another hobby."

I close the door behind her and hug the big book of obits. I feel like I'm getting back to being me. It's hard, but it's definitely getting easier to fight the worry.

*

MY JOURNAL STAYS IN the car when Dad drops me off in front of Hannah's house. Before I get to the door my phone buzzes. It's a text from Ryan with a link to the video of Sebastian's winning slam poem called "The Sea." It already has 1,000 hits online. I smile. My next slam poem is already written. But for now, it's just for me.

The truck beeps loudly as it backs into the driveway. It's moving day. Hannah's dad got a job at The Big Red Tomato, a new Italian restaurant in Seattle. Hannah comes running out. We hug and I try not to count or cry.

We go upstairs into Hannah's room and tuck ourselves safely on the floor of her closet, thankfully hidden from the chaos. Our hands clasp. My silent tears roll down my cheeks.

"Did you bring the stuff?" she asks. Her voice cracks.

"Yes, but first, I have a present for you." I slowly take the plastic bag out of my backpack, thankful it still has water in it. "Meet Max."

The bright blue Siamese fighting fish swims in circles at the sound of his name. Or my voice. Or maybe that's just what Siamese fighting fish do.

"Oh, Molly. He's beautiful." She slips Max into Fred's old bowl.

"Now, to the other stuff."

"Wait. I have a present, too." Hannah hands me a check.

I don't understand what this is.

"I came in second in the business contest."

"Hannah, that's amazing."

"Since my dad got a job, I decided to do something else with my winnings."

I look at the check in my hand. It's made out to the OCD Foundation.

We hug tight. Hannah and me are Hannah and me again.

"And because I can't leave with a guilty conscience, I told Mrs. Melvin I used her money for the contest entrance fee."

"What happened?"

"She said she meant to give me the fifty all along."

I decided not to remind her that I *did* suggest just asking Mrs. Melvin first.

"Now, what did you bring?" she asks.

"I brought our third-grade class photo where we're holding hands dressed as sunflowers, the medals I won at Color Day for coming in first place in my first race, my peach lip gloss, a box of sixty-four-count crayons, my Bazooka Joe fortune, my glass piglet, the photograph of us with our braces and frizzy hair at the fifth-grade summer picnic," I say.

"You've never had frizzy hair."

"Okay, maybe that was just you." I smile.

"Anything else?"

"The gimp keychain you made me at camp, and four Thin Mints."

"We're going to put the Thin Mints in?"

"No, we're going to eat them." I hand her two and eat the other two.

"What did you find?" I ask.

"My first-ever business plan for Lemonade on Laurel Lane and the drawing you made for me when Goldilocks died."

"You were so sad about that fish. You cried for three days straight. I was so thankful when you got Fred."

"I also put in the anklets we got at the carnival after we rode the upside-down roller coaster," she says.

"And you threw up all over the sidewalk."

"Yes, there was that. Thanks for reminding me. Anyway, I put in *Eloise*, the book we read every night you slept over, two red-and-white-striped circle mints from the last time we ate at Mandarin Gourmet, and two braided Color Me Bracelets. A blue-red-and-yellow one for each of us."

"I think we should include a note." I grab a piece of paper from her *Hannah Levine* pad. One of the few things that isn't packed yet. "This way when we dig it up in ten or twenty years, there will be a letter from the now, younger us to the later, older us."

We work on the letter for a while. I can hear Hannah's dad calling to the movers to be careful of their heads hitting the low ceilings and warning them of the fragility of his antique gnome collection.

February 1, 2014
Dear older Molly and Hannah,
   Hi. You're reading this because you dug up our time capsule. We hope you are both great and together. So funny to think you may be married, with kids even. We are twelve. Our plan: We're going to visit every summer, room together in college, and then rule the world. Kidding about the ruling-the-world part. We're hopeful that by the time you read this, Molly will be a famous slam poet (and not counting or organizing anymore) and Hannah will be the owner of a very cool business.

We're sad to be separating, for now, but we promise we are going to, not away from. And remember the promise. If you, the older versions of us, dig up this capsule, you will need to bury a new one and visit it again in another ten years.

Much love,
Hannah and Molly

I fold the letter into three (not four) sections and stuff it into an envelope marked *Hannah and Molly in the future*. For our time capsule, Hannah set aside a shoe box that wasn't going to Seattle. The plan is to bury the box next to the oak tree in the park at the top of Queens Hill.

"Seattle's not that far," I say as Hannah turns away from me. I see a tear slip down her cheek as she tapes the box closed. "It's a direct flight. Some bad airplane food, a horror movie, and you're practically landing." She gives me the same fake smile she gave me when she had to get her appendix out and was going to miss the school play. Rebecca Jones was Hannah's happy understudy who got to be Alice in *Alice in Wonderland*.

"You're right. My dad already said I could visit as

soon as school was over. Maybe we could split the summer. Half in Seattle and half in Lantern," Hannah says.

"I'd love that." The doors of the moving van slam
closed.

"Hannah, it's time," her dad calls up the stairs.

50

buried

HANNAH AND I WERE supposed to do this together, but we ran out of time. Something about the snow and traffic and needing to be sure they didn't miss their flight. I put on my boots and traipse up the hill with Oscar, a shovel, and the box.

My fingers are numb by the time I get to the top of Queens Hill. Hannah texted last night when she got to her new house. No more Facebook messages. When Dad found out about Lynx, he closed the account after a parenting moment that sounded like an *Ask Maggie* column.

Hannah had me video chat with her so she could show me around her new house. It's red brick with a black double door and a lawn. It sits next to a lake, and a *gaggle* of geese ate the seed off her front lawn while we talked. It was a little hard to hear over their squawking. Her room is decorated just like her old room—tulip yellow and pomegranate red. She zoomed in on a photo of the two of us at camp she has on her desk next to Max and her copy of *E. B.'s Rules to Becoming a Successful Businesswoman.* Then she showed me her idea room, which was actually a corner of the basement that her dad set up for her to work on her business plans. She seemed happy and sad at the same time. Before she hung up she said, "Miss you, Mol."

"Miss you too, Hannah." Saying goodbye to her was one of the hardest things I've ever had to do. It was on the list with saying goodbye to Mom and stopping all my weird stuff.

I grab the shovel out of the bag and begin to dig at our chosen spot by the tree. Dr. G.'s idea. Oscar runs around in the snow, searching for a stick to fetch. I grab one off the ground and toss it to him. I go back to digging. Digging is hard, mostly because it involves dirt and because I can't make a hole deep enough for our capsule. The ground's too hard. And uncooperative. Not completely frozen, but it doesn't matter. I keep at the same spot, but it isn't working. I lure Oscar over and put the stick in the hole. He's a good digger, but gets distracted easily. He picks up the stick with his teeth and runs away.

I have another idea.

"Come on, Oscar. We'll be back." I drop the shovel and he follows me as we head home.

Kate and Ian are in the kitchen eating from a gallon container of coffee ice cream.

"Want some?" Ian asks.

I shake my head no. "But I could use some help. Feel like digging?"

They grab their boots and the three of us trudge back up to the top of Queens Hill.

"What's in the box?" Ian shakes it.

"Stuff from Hannah and me."

"Why are you burying your stuff in the ground?" he wants to know.

"It's a time capsule," Kate says. "I think it's cool."

I smile. Since my total meltdown there have been more three-of-us moments. It feels nice. Odd. But nice.

Kate and Ian and I all start digging. After about fifteen minutes we've dug a hole large enough for the box.

"Should we say something or do some sort of ceremony before you put it in the ground?" Kate asks.

I shrug. "Don't know. Maybe just, 'See you in ten years.'"

I cover the box with dirt and snow, snap a picture of the spot with my phone, and send it to Hannah and Dr. G. (part of my homework). Kate and I sit down next to the buried capsule while Ian tries to climb the tree.

"You okay?" she asks.

"Yeah. No. I don't know. I'm just really going to miss Hannah."

I wait for the numbers, but they don't come. Maybe this is the start of something new. Maybe Dr. G. is right. Things are getting better.

Kate puts her muddy hand on top of mine.

I let her.

51

three days shy
of being thirteen

I WALK INTO THE OCD group meeting and see Parker Ray
by the chips at the table near the windows. He smiles
and gives me a thumbs-up. Translation—no counting,
just eating chips. I smile. Devon starts group. This week
there are fifteen of us. The new girl's pale frightened face
is a stark contrast to her raw hands. She sits on them
when she notices me. I want to put my arm around her
and tell her she's going to be okay.

My metal chair makes a loud noise when I stand. I'm
ready, but still totally nervous. This is a first. Another
first. I clear my throat like there's something in it, but
really I just need another second to catch my breath.

Inhale. Exhale.

"I want to share something I wrote in my journal."

Parker Ray's applause fills the quiet space.

I start:

Beyond the darkness
There is light
Beyond the fear
There is hope
Beyond the perfection
There is me.

Imperfect and beautiful
Me.

When I finish reading my poem, I say, "I'm Molly. I'm three days shy of being thirteen, and I have five letters in my name."

experts consulted

DR. KATHLEEN TRAINOR, FOUNDER of the TRAINOR Center, has treated children and adolescents with anxiety-based disorders using the latest in evidence-based approaches for more than thirty years. Her practice, which focuses on cognitive behavioral therapy (CBT), is tailored to meet each child's needs. A senior psychologist on the staff of the Child Psychiatry Clinic at Massachusetts General Hospital, Dr. Trainor holds a master's degree in social work and a doctorate in clinical psychology; she has been on the faculty of Harvard Medical School for more than twenty years. Since 1988, Dr. Trainor has been a private-practice psychotherapist, providing adult, adolescent, couple, and family CBT in solo practice, first as a licensed independent certified social worker (LICSW) and then as a licensed psychologist. Dr. Trainor presents to professional and community groups in the areas of cognitive behavioral treatment of anxiety disorders, Obsessive-Compulsive Disorder, Tourette's syndrome, autism, trichotillomania, and more. She also provides training and consultations in schools and to therapists in various clinical settings. She is known for her unique and widely used 7-Step TRAINOR Method, and her long-awaited book, *Calming Your Anxious Child: Words to Say and Things to Do*, is now available.

Paul Cannistraro, MD, is a psychiatrist in private practice in Cambridge, Massachusetts. He is the former director of clinical psychopharmacology at the Massachusetts General Hospital Obsessive-Compulsive Disorders Clinic. He has published numerous neuroimaging and clinical research studies and continues to lecture on pharmacological treatments for OCD and related disorders.

resources consulted

Fitzgibbons, Lee, Ph.D., and Cherry Pedrick, RN. *Helping Your Child with OCD: A Workbook for Parents of Children with Obsessive-Compulsive Disorder.* Oakland, CA: New Harbinger Publications, Inc., 2003.

Goodman, W. K., L. H. Price, S. A. Rasmussen, et al. "Y-BOC Symptom Checklist," adapted from "The Yale-Brown Obsessive Compulsive Scale." *Archives of General Psychiatry* 46 (1989): 1006–1011.

How to Help Your Child with OCD: A Parent's Guide to OCD. Chicago: Obsessive Compulsive Foundation of Metropolitan Chicago, 2006.

How to Recognize and Respond to OCD in School-Age Children. OC Foundation, Inc. Video.

International OCD Foundation. iocdf.org. This site lists
numerous resources for parents, kids, and professionals
to consult.

Jake's Story and the Kids Panel. OC Foundation, Inc. Video.

Wagner, Aureen Pinto, Ph.D. *What to Do When Your Child
Has Obsessive-Compulsive Disorder.* Apex, NC: Lighthouse
Press, Inc., 2002.

acknowledgments

THANK YOU SEEMS LIKE an enormous understatement. My journey to *Finding Perfect* was thirteen years, many reads, dozens of revisions, lots of wine/Twizzlers/flowers, and hundreds of hugs in the making. Looking back, however, I wouldn't change a single thing. I learned that writing a novel is a lot like hiking a switchback on a mountain. You know it's a long way down, but chances are you're going to encounter some gems along the way. And that I did.

To my greatest gems—my husband, James, and my boys, Joshua and Gregory—where do I even begin? I'm not sure you will ever truly know the depths of my love and gratitude. Without you, this book would never have gotten off my $8\frac{1}{2} \times 11$ computer paper. The three of you believed in me unconditionally. Year after year. You never wavered. Not once. I love you all with all of me.

To the rest of my amazing family, I am so grateful for all of you. The unconditional love, the unwavering support, and, of course, the wine. Thank you all on both coasts for believing in me as I navigated down this long and winding path. Love you all more than you know!

Tricia Lawrence, agent and friend extraordinaire, to you I say a deep-in-the-center-of-my-heart thank-you! You said we'd get to YES together. You said *FP* would find a home. And how right you were. I am so grateful for your confidence in me, your intuition, your kindness, and your humor. You helped make all of this possible.

To my most wonderful FSG editor, Angie Chen, there may be no words that accurately reflect the bounds of my gratitude. From the moment you told me that you loved Molly, I knew *Finding Perfect* and I had found a home. Your insight and edits helped make Molly's story complete. You were my own personal book whisperer! To the wonderfully talented, smart, and insightful Joy Peskin, I am so grateful that Molly and I have you at the helm as I navigate the next part of this journey. You are a true rock star among editors. How lucky I am to be working with you! And to the FSG team who worked to bring this book from my computer to the bookshelf, please know I am beyond appreciative for your creativity and dedication.

To my wonderful girlfriends who rooted for me, listened to my book-talk, cheered loudly when *FP* found its place in the world, and loved me all the way, I love you all like sisters.

Sarah Aronson, you have been a cherished mentor/ teacher/friend through the years. You will forever have a special place in my books and my heart.

The EMLA family, love you guys. Seriously, I could not have asked for a more gracious, supportive, caring, smart, talented writing community to be a part of. How lucky I am!

Dr. Trainor and Dr. Cannistraro, thank you for sharing your knowledge with me. It was so important to me that Molly's manifestation of and treatment for OCD be authentic. Your input was invaluable. And, Dr. Trainor, thank you for going above and beyond over the period of three years, reading my manuscript, answering my questions, and meeting with me. Molly and I both thank you!

Nancy Tupper Ling, I so appreciate the time you took to edit/guide/discuss the ways of poetry. I am grateful that I had a true poet to lean on.

To my readers and former crit group, your input over the many drafts was invaluable and always appreciated.

To those who are no longer with me. To my mom, I thank you for all of it. You taught me how to love unconditionally, be courageous, and color outside the lines. You made me feel like I could do anything. I love you beyond and miss you every single day. To my father-in-law, I thank you for always loving me and cheering me on. And to my almost-102-year-old Gram, I hope you're enjoying your Harvey's Bristol Cream as you read my story.

So to all who shared this switchback with me, your endless encouragement and confidence in me allowed me to uncover the last gem along my journey—never stop believing in your dreams. From the bottom of my heart, I thank you.

I.

Am.

Beyond.

Grateful.